A Fruitful Vine

DISTRIBUTED BY
Choice Books
Salunga, PA 17538
We Welcome Your Response

Miriam's Journal

Also by Carrie Bender
Whispering Brook Farm

Carrie Bender

A Fruitful Vine

HERALD PRESS
Scottdale, Pennsylvania
Waterloo, Ontario

Library of Congress Cataloging-in-Publication Data
Bender, Carrie
    A fruitful vine / by Carrie Bender.
        p. cm.
    ISBN 0-8361-3613-6 (alk. paper)
    I. Title
PS3552.E53845F78 1993   92-36425
                                                              CIP

The paper used in this publication is recycled and meets the minimum
requirements of American National Standard for Information
Sciences—Permanence of Paper for Printed Library Materials, ANSI
Z39.48-1984.

Scripture quotations and allusions imbedded in the text are based on
the *King James Version of the Holy Bible*, with some adaptation to
current English usage. For a list of references, see pages 189-190.

A FRUITFUL VINE
Copyright © 1993 by Herald Press, Scottdale, Pa. 15683
    Published simultaneously in Canada by Herald Press,
    Waterloo, Ont. N2L 6H7. All rights reserved
Library of Congress Catalog Number: 92-36425
International Standard Book Number: 0-8361-3613-6
Printed in the United States of America
Book design by Paula M. Johnson
Inside illustrations by Susan E. Haas
Divider pages and cover art by Joy Dunn Keenan

02 01 00 99 98 97 96 95 10 9 8 7 6 5
27,000 copies in print

To my family,
without whom this book
could not have been written

Note
This story is fiction.
Any resemblance to persons living
or dead is purely coincidental.

Contents

YEAR ONE

Alone

*M*y fortieth birthday! I'm sitting on a rock out here in the meadow. The creek runs nearby, and a fragrant early morning breeze is dancing over the nearby hayfield, wafting its sweetness to me and rustling the leaves overhead. There is a splendid, rose-tinted sunrise in the east. The creek is talking and gurgling as it flows over the rocks. But my heart seems dead to all this beauty.

There's just a heavy weight where my heart ought to be. I've carried that load ever since Mother died last week. Now I am alone—so alone! Maybe it will help me to write down some of my feelings day by day.

This will not be an ordinary diary—the kind you start on New Year's Day and write what you work and do every day. Instead, in this journal I can safely pour out my feelings when I've no one else to tell them to. I'll also do some sketching, although I haven't much talent for either writing or drawing.

Yes, today I, Miriam Miller, am forty years old. I don't feel old yet. My hair is still black, I'm slender, and I've no noticeable wrinkles yet. I still feel like a young girl inside. Maybe it's because I've never been married.

Since the funeral, I haven't been alone much. Yet there is always the painful awareness that now I *am* alone. When Dad died of a heart attack five years ago, it was hard to bear, but I still had Mother. She often talked about how they had resigned themselves to being a childless couple. Then when they were both forty-three, I was born.

I suppose I brought a lot of joy into the household, but I was an only child, and I missed the fun of a large family. Now I feel it even more keenly. If I'd have brothers and sisters, I wouldn't be so alone. And in this community I have no uncles or aunts, either.

I used to dream of having a husband and a home of our own, a houseful of children and laughter and songs. But those dreams died a long time ago. Dad was completely bedfast for four years and needed so much care that I hadn't much time to think about what I was missing.

When Dad was gone, Mother seemed to lose her will to live, and I had to do almost everything for her. I often longed to be free to travel or go on shopping trips, to take long, long walks—to have time to do whatever I wished.

Now that I *am* free, I feel alone—frightened to face the future. Mother was good and kind, my best friend. Now I can hardly see to write through my tears. . . . 🌿

July 28

*A*s for God, his way is perfect: the word of the Lord is tried, he is a buckler to all those that trust in him. These last few weeks have been hard ones indeed, but my Savior has been with me every step of the way. I have learned the real meaning of Christ's words, "I will never leave you nor forsake you." He has been continually with me. Fellowship with him has become more meaningful than ever.

My dear friend Mary, who also is single, wrote me a letter: "The loving heavenly Father is your best friend. He gave his only begotten Son for you. He will bless you and keep you. He will draw you to himself, fill you with his Spirit, give you courage for every struggle, victory for every sin, a blessing for every cross.

"Just surrender your all to your heavenly Father. Give God your fears, your troubles, and your loneliness. He wants to carry them for you, and he will never leave you nor forsake you."

Those words helped me so much. My eyes watered as I read them.

What a surprise I had on my birthday when the mail carrier left me over eighty cards! Lots of them included letters. People have been good to me, and I feel as if there is yet a balm in Gilead.

July 29

*B*efore us is a future
all unknown—a path untrod.
Beside us is a friend well-loved and known—
that friend is God. (Unknown)

I've come to the creek again with my journal to try to sort out my thoughts. It's such a sweet and friendly day. How dear the trees are! How beautiful the creek! I'm sitting on an old mossy log, and some tiny green ferns are growing on either side. A beam of sunshine streams through the leaves and shines far down into the water in interesting ripples.

Ever since Mother died, I've been waiting for guidance, tossing around my choices for the future. I have aspirations to be an influence for good to someone, to do some self-sacrificing work for the Lord, to lend a helping hand to someone in need, to give an encouraging word and smile, to be a beam of light in this dark world. But all I can think of is to be a schoolteacher, and I'm afraid I'm too old to start on such a career.

In my daily devotional booklet is an article about guidance. I'll write down some pointers as I remember them in order to reinforce them in my mind: 1. We must realize that we lack wisdom. 2. We must really desire to know God's way and be fully willing to do his will. 3. We must ask and definitely pray for guidance. 4. We must confidently expect guidance, even though only a step is made clear at a time. 5. We must follow step by step as the guidance comes—as to where to go, and where not to go; what to do, and what not to do; and what to say, and what not to say.

In time God's guidance becomes clear. Many are tortured, being unsure. Go to God and say, "Here I am, heavenly Father. I am willing to do your will—but show me what it is." If you are ready to do God's will, he will show the way. You need not and ought not try something until God does make it clear.

Those are comforting thoughts. "They also serve who only stand and wait" (J. Milton).

Twilight is stealing over the sweetness of summer-scented meadows and field. My heart is full and overflowing with joy and the knowledge that if I surrender everything to God, he will lead me step by step. 🌾

*T*oday I received a letter from widow Anna Beiler. Her daughter, Elizabeth, died a year ago. She was married to Isaac Bontrager and had a newborn baby.

Anna's single daughter, Rebecca, was keeping house for Isaac and caring for the baby, but now she's getting married, so they're looking for another housekeeper. She wondered if I'd consider taking the job.

I am really excited about it, but I want to pray over it some more. Is it God's will for me to go?

August 15

*W*ell, here I am at my new job of being a housekeeper for Isaac. I'm upstairs in my room. Isaac has taken one-year-old Matthew along to the barn with him. I can hardly believe I'm really here. Things happened so fast, and everything fell into place so smoothly! I'm sure God was planning it all.

A soft evening breeze is flowing in the window, stirring the curtains. Since I've been here, the weather has been perfect. Blue, blue skies. Not too hot and not too cold, sunshine and breezes. But since it's August, this is probably only a brief respite from the heat.

I like this farm, the neat white house trimmed with green, the picket fence, and the trees. We're in a rather long lane, lined with trees. Even this late in the summer, lots of songbirds are around. How must it sound in the spring?

Little Matthew is such a sweet baby, chubby, and beginning to toddle around, lisping baby sounds. I can see that Isaac simply adores him. It's a year now since Elizabeth died, and I think his sorrow is healed—at least outwardly. He's fun to work with, and he laughs and teases. This is an easy job, and I thank God for giving it to me.

Sometimes I even allow myself to think what it would be like if I'd also be twenty-four, and be his wife and Matthew's mother. I like it so much here. Is there something in the air, or what, that makes me feel full to the brim of the joy of life? It's so good to feel needed again!

Caring for the baby is such a pleasure. Yesterday he wrapped his chubby little arms around my neck and hugged me. A newly awakened, sweet thrill of tender motherhood feelings stirred my heart. I'll cherish that feeling for all time. 🌿

September 2

I'm sitting and writing in my spotless kitchen—already this kitchen seems so special and so mine. Outside it's pouring down rain, and Isaac is on the floor playing with Matthew. I enjoy watching them, and it does my heart good to hear them both laughing.

If it wouldn't be raining, we'd probably be out taking a drive, something we do almost every evening. Isaac is a horse trainer, and the horses need exercise every day. When Matthew and I go along, he takes one of the safer horses, one well-broken and almost ready to go to the new owner. I wouldn't ride along for anything with some of those wild broncos he's just starting to tame.

Even just watching from the kitchen, my heart beats wildly and I hold my breath when I see a horse rear on its hind legs or throw itself to the ground. But Isaac always seems to know what to do. When I fear for his safety and wonder what I would do if he'd get hurt, I remind myself that God controls everything, even a wild horse.

Just now Matthew grabbed hold of Isaac's hair and yanked. Isaac shook his head from side to side, and I had to laugh at the face he made. He really looked funny. Generally, he's not bad to look at—brown, wavy hair, a frank, clean-cut look, tall, and well built. The longer I'm here, the more I realize what a decent chap he is.

We've had some long talks, sharing our feelings and our thoughts about certain principles. It's been a long time since I've opened my heart to anyone like this. Since I'm so much older than Isaac, he seems to have me on a pedestal of being infinitely wise. He asks questions that I think that he, being a man, would be able to answer better than I. But I gallantly make a try at it.

Today he told me something that sent a queer stab of jealousy into my heart. He confided that for the last few months he's been seeing a girl, Priscilla Kauffman. I hadn't the slightest idea that was going on, but now that he told me, I realize I should have known. A few times he went away in the evening, all spruced up and whistling a happy tune. She's eighteen years old and not allowed to get married before spring.

How short that will make my stay here! I must keep reminding myself not to get too attached to Matthew and Isaac; that would only make my leaving them all the harder. But in my heart I know I am already hopelessly attached to them. It will be unbearably hard to leave. I claim

God's promise: My child, my grace is sufficient for you. And I know it will be. This won't be the first time I've gone through a hard thing. ✍

*T*he days are passing by in delicious succession. On the way to church this morning, it was inexpressibly beautiful after the rain. Little rainbows sparkled on the leaves and grass, and the drenched shrubbery gave out spicy odors. Delightful mists hovered over the harvest fields, and the air was fragrant and scented. The horse lifted his head as if sniffing the air, and he raised his feet so high that I believe he felt like prancing.

I like attending the church in this district, I like the people, and I like the preachers, Dan and Amos. Because I am a newcomer, as soon as I step into the yard, Mamie Lapp comes over to me and hovers around until we're ready to file into the house and be seated. Then she takes me by the hand and smilingly leads me to sit with her. Although she's just a few months older than I, she has the mind of a child, and at first it disconcerted me a bit, but now I don't mind.

Last Sunday Isaac said to me, "If I were you, I wouldn't hang around Mamie so much."

"Why not?" I asked.

"What will people think? Perhaps they'll get an idea you're a little like her."

I laughed heartily. "I don't care a bit what people think. Since it makes Mamie so happy, I'm going to continue to be her friend."

And now for the exciting news. On Wednesday Priscilla is coming for supper. I'm so excited, I can hardly wait. I haven't met her yet because she attends church in another district.

Isaac had gone to see her on Friday evening, and since then he seemed quiet and perturbed about something. Last night he told me why. Priscilla has a cantankerous old dad, who doesn't attend any church now and is an outright atheist. He openly says he doesn't believe in God and that the Bible is a farce and that all religious people are either nuts or hypocrites. She and her mom follow the rules of the church and serve him meals at a separate table.

Priscilla is an only child. When her dad discovered that Isaac was dating his daughter, he flew into a rage and forbade him ever to set foot on the place again. He is often away all evening until after midnight, but on Friday evening he came home earlier. For the first time, he found out about Isaac. I do feel sorry for Isaac and hope everything will work out all right for him.

At church, Preacher Dan had the text about the ten virgins. How sad that the door was closed to the five! Yet I treasure the glorious thought that I am a part of the church of God—the bride of Christ!

A few sentences that Dan stressed stand out in my memory: Live so as to please your heavenly bridegroom. Flee from anything and everything that would tend to rob you of your love for Christ. Never allow yourself in any way to grieve the Holy Spirit, in whom we are sealed unto the day of redemption.

I am going to pray for Priscilla's dad. How unutterably sad! I cried myself to sleep last night just thinking about the whole situation. ❧

*W*hat a day this has been! I flew around all day getting the house and yard absolutely spotless. I baked shoofly pies, prepared *Schnitz un Knepp,* and beheaded a rooster and dressed it, ready for the roasting pan tomorrow.

I could see that Isaac was pleased, and he lent me a hand whenever he came in. After supper he took Matthew along outside so I could get the rest of my work done faster. Everything had to be perfect for Priscilla.

I'm invited to an all-day quilting at Polly Mast's house tomorrow, so I have to work on ahead. I'll bring Priscilla along home after that, and she can help me get supper ready.

I had just started to wash windows when there was a knock at the door. It was the neighbor boy with a note for me. On the slip of paper was a telephone number, and the note asked me to call that number as soon as possible. I hurried as fast as I could to the neighbor's, my heart thumping. What could possibly be wrong? Had there been a bad accident, or did someone die?

By the time I arrived at the phone, I was so breathless that I couldn't talk right away. An unfamiliar voice said, "Hello, this is Priscilla Kauffman's mother. Is this Miriam?"

She cleared her throat nervously and talked so jerkily that I could hardly follow her, but finally I understood what she was trying to say.

"I want you to keep an eye on my daughter tomorrow night," she demanded gratingly. "Don't let her and the widower be alone. You be the chaperone! Can you promise me you'll do that?"

"Now wait a minute!" I protested. "I can't promise you anything like that. What if Isaac wouldn't want it? I'm only working for him, you know."

She then resorted to begging. "Please do that for me." Her voice was teary. "Please."

I interrupted, "I don't think you have anything to worry about. Isaac is a real decent fellow."

She quickly said, "I'm not saying he isn't. It's *her* I don't trust. She's broken too many hearts already."

I wondered why she would say that. Finally I promised I'd do as she wished, but only if Isaac agreed. She had to be satisfied with that and soon hung up.

On the way home I had a wild desire to laugh hysterically. *Me*, a chaperone of a dating couple! It sure wouldn't be the nicest job!

Yet it was a golden evening, a gorgeous sunset in the west, and a song sparrow sang its sweet tune—perhaps to cheer me. I sent a prayer heavenward that somehow everything would work out all right.

When I got home, I didn't feel like finishing the windows. Instead, I played with Matthew all evening. We had rollicking fun with peekaboo and pat-a-cake. Then I gave him his bath and rocked him to sleep. Now I have to go downstairs and have a talk with Isaac when he comes in. 🌿

September 17

*F*inally the excitement of the day has ceased. The house is quiet, and the night insects and crickets are chorusing.

First I'll write about the quilting. Polly Mast is a maiden lady, a little older than I am. She has a cute, quaint little home of her own with a blue roof, trim, and shutters. It's surrounded by a blue picket fence.

The yard and garden are full of flowers, and a brook flows through a corner of it. There's a winding walk up to the house bordered on either side by flowers, and at the end of the walk there's a cute swinging gate, and it's blue, too!

At the quilting Lovina Mast asked about the blue gate. At first I didn't realize she was teasing, and Polly didn't either. According to Lovina, a blue gate means there's a marriageable daughter in the house.

"Really?" exclaimed Polly. "But I don't have a marriageable daughter."

Everyone burst out laughing at that.

Then Lovina explained, "*You're* the marriageable daughter!"

I heartily agreed with that statement. Polly is pleasant-faced and round-cheeked and jolly, warm and comfortable besides. I knew right away I was going to like her.

Being at a quilting is a good way to get to know the neighborhood women and also to find out all kinds of gossip—news, I should say. Polly had two quilts in frames. I was there early and didn't see who gathered around the other quilt in the next room. I was wondering so much whether Priscilla was there.

At lunchtime Polly called us to a luscious dinner of fried chicken, mashed potatoes and gravy, homemade noodles, succotash, lettuce salad, ice-cream pie with strawberry topping, and chiffon marble cake. I was sitting there enjoying the feast when Polly came and pointed out Priscilla to me. I nearly gasped. Isaac hadn't told me that she was such a lady! Her hair is blond, and her features are as perfect as a painted china doll's face. Her skin is creamy white. No wonder Isaac is attracted to her!

Priscilla was laughing and talking, and I just stared in

fascination. But back to quilting I went, until four o'clock. We finally had our quilt finished—a lovely Double Wedding Ring. Priscilla came over to see it, and by the big smile she gave me, I knew she'd been told who I was.

Soon afterward, they completed the other quilt, a Dresden Plate, in shades of blue. The ladies began to leave. Priscilla and I walked home to Isaac's—it's only a mile or so. Finally we had a chance to get acquainted. She certainly is not shy and chatted almost nonstop.

Isaac was still finishing his chores. He came out of the barn with smiles, leading Matthew by the hand, and walked over to meet us. They sat on the porch swing, talking, while I prepared supper. After a while Priscilla and Matthew came in.

"Oh, I hope Iky isn't mad," she said.

That's funny, I thought. She's the only one I ever heard calling him Iky.

"He asked if I want to go along to the barn and see the horses while he finishes the chores. But I didn't want to. I can't stand barn smells." She pretended to shiver.

"Oh, didn't you grow up on a farm?" I asked.

"No way! And am I ever glad!"

Priscilla didn't offer to help with the supper or to entertain Matthew, either. Instead, she walked around examining the kitchen. On the stand beside the sofa was Isaac's Bible with his name printed on it.

"What's this?"

I looked at her strangely. Surely she knew what a Bible was!

"Oh, it's a Bible. What does he have it lying here for?"

"He reads aloud to us every evening," I explained. I could see she was genuinely shocked.

"I thought Bibles were only for church," she commented. "We aren't allowed to have a Bible in our home."

"But your mother . . . surely she has a Bible, doesn't she?"

"Not that I know of."

"But didn't she tell you Bible stories and help you memorize some verses?"

"Well, she did some when I was young. But then my dad left the church, and now my only chance to hear the Bible is on Sunday morning."

I felt so sorry for the girl. She and her mother are church members, but I have to wonder if she understands. She seems so shallow and flippant. Is there a capacity for understanding there, or is she just a brainless beauty?

Then I went over to the sofa with Matthew and changed his messy diaper. Suddenly she squealed and ran across the room, holding her nose. That really exasperated me.

"You'd better have him trained before we get married!" she blurted out. "I wouldn't change a soiled diaper for anything."

"Just what would you do if you'd have a baby of your own?" I asked, a trifle hotly.

"Oh, I'm never having one!" she quickly responded.

"Never having any children!" I could hardly believe her. "What would Isaac think? I know he loves children and wants a houseful of them."

"Oh, don't tell him," she pleaded, looking frightened.

"I most certainly will tell him if you don't tell him yourself," I retorted.

Priscilla laughed gaily, then, and said, "Oh, I was only kidding. Can't you tell when someone's kidding? Please don't take me seriously, and don't mention this to Isaac. I really was only kidding. I'll gladly have sixteen or twenty."

She kept up a bright chatter all during supper and helped wash the dishes afterward. Isaac and Priscilla then sat on the porch swing again.

I was writing letters to friends at the kitchen table and could only hear the murmur of their voices and an occasional laugh. When I had told Isaac of the call made by Priscilla's mother, I could tell he was vexed at her for requesting me to check on them. Isaac had told me, "No need for you to chaperone us; Matthew will be our chaperone."

For a while I had debated about whether or not I should tell Isaac what Priscilla's mom had said about her having broken enough hearts. Finally I told him. I thought it gave him a jolt, but then he shrugged it off. Isaac just said, "Priscilla's mom is having mental problems. That's why she's so nervous about us and why she imagines things that aren't so. You really can't blame her with a husband like that, can you?"

At eight that evening, Priscilla's neighbor picked her up to take her home, and Isaac came into the kitchen and sat on a chair across the table from me.

"Well, tell me exactly what you think of Priscilla," he began, half shyly and half eagerly.

I bit my lip. I wanted ever so much to tell him to please, please not marry her, that she is immature, selfish, shallow, flippant, and that I doubt that's she's intelligent enough to understand what it means to be a Christian. But I couldn't say any of it. I was afraid Isaac would think I was just saying it because I was jealous. So I merely said, "She has a lot of growing up to do, hasn't she?"

"She sure does," he agreed. "Maybe I can help her to

grow up. She never had a chance with such a dad."

I could tell that he was already caught—hook, line, and sinker. It gives me a sinking feeling inside, but perhaps he said the truth. Maybe with a good husband like him, she'll mature, and with her beauty, be a gracious wife for him.

At any rate, I'll take it to the Lord in prayer. I think a lot of Isaac, and I'd sure hate to see him get hurt. ❧

I didn't realize it would get so warm here near the end of September. It sure was a scorcher today. Isaac heard from one of the neighbors that Allen Keim's got a truckload of ice-cream that they're selling for ten cents a box, probably because the expiration date has passed.

Suddenly Isaac was hungry for ice cream. "Would you mind driving over to Allen's to get some ice cream?"

I decided that if he asks me to drive eight miles in this heat on a Saturday afternoon, maybe I'd better go, although it *ferlated* (disgusted) me awfully.

He hitched up faithful Beauty, and I started off. When I passed the IGA store in town, I was tempted to stop and get all the ice cream he wants and pay with my own money. But I was afraid he wouldn't like that, so I drove on.

At Allen's place, I met the ice-cream truck coming out the lane. As I drove up to the tie railing, Allen came out of the barn and told me, "I'm sorry, but the last box of ice cream was sold just ten minutes ago."

What a disappointment! But there was nothing to do but turn around and go home. I consoled myself with the thought that I could still get ice cream at the IGA store on the way back. But, alas, just as I drove up, the store was being locked. I was too late again.

To top it off, when I reached home, Isaac told me that I had missed company. Uncle Peter and Aunt Fannie had stopped in, en route to Ohio, and waited for me, hoping I'd return before they'd have to leave to catch a bus. They left just fifteen minutes before I returned.

When I was alone I had a good cry. ❀

October 15

*T*hese days I've been busy doing housecleaning, raking leaves, and helping with the cornhusking. This afternoon I was husking alone because Isaac has a sore hand. It was a beautiful October day, blue of sky and golden with sunshine. A crisp wind was blowing up over the fields, and a splendid mass of fluffy clouds heaped up over the distant mountains.

I was in a back field, and from there I could see no buildings or roads, not even a telephone line. It was easy to imagine that I was all alone in the world. After a while I began to get the feeling that maybe all the other people had been raptured up and I was the only one left in this world. How silly of me! It even took me a while to force myself to snap out of it.

Then I worked happily away, sometimes singing, sometimes praying, feeling close to God, with an abiding sense of his nearness comforting me. I will lift my eyes unto the hills, from whence comes my help. My help comes from the Lord, who made heaven and earth. ❀

*T*his afternoon I went to visit Polly Mast. It was truly delightful, and now I regard her as a bosom friend. I came home, convinced afresh that this is an interesting world and that life is a wonderful thing. To be in the company of a man is all right for a while, but a woman needs to have a chat with another woman every once in a while, too.

Polly showed me through her cozy little house, her hooked rugs, bookcases filled with interesting books, then out to her yard and garden. We sat on a blanket beside the brook, talking to our heart's content.

The shadows were long and lazy among the trees bordering the brook, and an autumn wind whispered dreamily through the dried leaves.

"Well, tell me about yourself," Polly suggested. "What did you do during your twenties and thirties? What are your dreams and ambitions? Were you ever in love?"

Sitting with my back against a tree, I told her all about myself. There's nothing I'd wish to hide from anyone. I even told her about Joe.

For six months Joe and I had dated each other, and then he moved to another community. We wrote to each other regularly at first, then his letters came further apart and finally quit altogether. A year later I found out why. He came back to visit with another girl at his side, and a short time later they were married. Such is life!

Then it was her turn. I was wiping away tears by the time she was finished. She had dated a boy named Calvin from age seventeen to twenty-one, and they were planning to get married. Two months before the planned wedding date, he was killed in a farm accident.

Two years later a guy named Leroy dated her. They had been going together for a year when he left the Amish church, begging her to go along, too. She chose, instead to remain steadfast to the faith.

"How could you bear so much sorrow?" I asked her.

She replied, "There's nothing on earth that heaven can't heal."

Polly would have made a perfect wife, to my way of thinking. Some things in this life are hard to understand! 🌿

November 3

*H*ow I cherish our evening drives through the crisp, fresh air, talking with Isaac and holding Matthew. Isaac enjoys them, too, and that is when he is most talkative. We can drive a long distance through the scenic countryside without meeting any traffic—so different from what I was used to.

Tonight as we were driving, I said to him, "Tell me about Elizabeth. How did she look? What was she like?"

His answer thrilled me. "She was a good Christian, just like you."

He couldn't have said anything else that would have made me happier.

Then he continued, "And she looked like an angel."

Neither of us spoke for a while, then, but I was thinking: Poor man! Now you'll be marrying a selfish brat. Of course I didn't say that!

Isaac is still going to see Priscilla, but they meet at a

neighbor's place. On Friday she'll be coming here again for supper.

Dear little Matthew! Will she love you and hold you and change your diaper? He was bouncing around on my lap, saying "horsie." Matthew is learning to say lots of new words. If she doesn't love him, I'll take him with me! But Isaac would never consent to that.

On Thursday, November 20, we're invited to Susie Raber and Henry Weaver's wedding. I'm looking forward to it. It's been a while since I've been at a wedding. Most other Amish people have lots and lots of relatives and are invited to several weddings each November, but it's a rare and special event for me.

The rest of the evening before I go to bed, I want to spend praying for Priscilla and Isaac. Happiness ought to be in my heart for them, but instead there's just an ache. Their courtship doesn't seem to be right or God's will. ✿

November 5

A terrible thing has happened, and I am shocked beyond words. Tonight we drove to the local farm market and livestock auction. Isaac had some things to put on the market, and he asked me to go along.

There were stand after stand of fruits, vegetables, crafts, meats, shoes, clothes, subs, cotton candy, and hot dogs. A blind man was playing his accordion. It got rather late because Isaac wanted to wait until his things were sold, so I wandered over to the auction barn. I was tired and longed for my bed. I guess I'm too old for such goings-on.

The auctioneering went on and on, and I began to get

drowsy. Suddenly I jerked wide awake. Right in front of me, arm in arm, a man and a girl came walking by. To my horror the girl was none other than Priscilla Kauffman!

She was smiling coquettishly up at him, almost prancing along, when suddenly she caught sight of me. She stopped short, gasped, and blurted out, "I never thought I'd see you here!"

I couldn't say a word. I tried, but no sound came out.

She walked on then, and away from the man. I was completely stunned. While I was searching for a place to sit down, Isaac came to say he was ready to go. He was white-faced and tight-lipped, and I knew he'd seen them.

All the way home he didn't say a word and neither did I—but I prayed aplenty.

Apparently the horse Isaac was driving wasn't as well broken as he thought, or else he wasn't used to being on the road in the dark. He was about as wild as could be. Yet I felt so numb that I wasn't even scared.

At the crossing he didn't want to stand, and lunged and reared. For a few awesome moments I thought he was go-

ing to fall backward on top of us, but then he started off on a rampage, and it was all Isaac could do to hold him in.

Later the horse shied into a ditch and almost upset the buggy. He balked at the next crossing and started backing. I thought, any minute now we'll be falling over a steep bank. But finally he leaped forward and nearly lifted the front buggy wheels off the pavement.

Now I'm in my bed, but I'm rather surprised that I'm still all in one piece!

Poor Isaac! I doubt whether there'll be any sleep for him tonight. I wonder if Priscilla will still be coming for supper tomorrow night as planned.

I'll try casting all my cares upon God, for he cares for us. Precious promise! 🌿

November 7

*P*riscilla came for supper, just as had been planned. She and Isaac went into the sitting room right away when she arrived, and Isaac shut the door.

I continued preparing supper, but I couldn't help but hear their voices. At first it was only a low murmur, then the voices got louder and louder. His was gruff and accusing, and hers tearful and pleading. Then loud sobs from her, and finally his voice low and soothing again.

My heart felt like a lead weight within. When they came out, she was all smiles again. So she had won!

I couldn't bring myself to say much all evening, and Isaac was on the quiet side, too. Only Priscilla kept up a stream of bright chatter all evening. Her driver came early, and Isaac put Matthew to bed. I made a pot of coffee, and we sat at the kitchen table.

"Did I do the right thing?" he asked wearily, stirring his coffee.

Well, if he wanted reassurance, he surely asked the wrong person, I thought.

"Oh, please, Isaac," I begged, "give her her walking papers. She isn't half good enough for you. She's lacking in character and hasn't the moral standards you do." I was almost surprised at my own vehemence.

He seemed terribly troubled and agitated. Without being aware of what he was doing, he ran his hand through his hair over and over until it stood straight up, giving him a wild appearance.

"But think of the upbringing she had," he protested quietly. "With parents like that, how could she have a chance? I'd like to give her a chance. Besides, I can't stop loving her."

I was thinking hard thoughts: Men are so stupid! so gullible! so weak! How I'd like to beat some sense into his head!

"I have to forgive her, don't I?" he went on. "Aren't we supposed to forgive seventy times seven?"

"Oh sure!" I agreed, almost indignantly. "Forgive her, yes! But that doesn't mean you have to marry her. Please reconsider, Isaac. I feel sure that somewhere God has a lovely girl he's preparing for you, one that has a good, sweet character and is a dedicated Christian. I don't want to see you get hurt. I want you to be happy. Pray about it some more."

With that, I came upstairs. Did I say too much? What if it's true that if he marries her and gives her a "chance," she'll blossom into a lovely, gracious Christian wife? What if he takes my advice and marries someone else, and it turns out to be an unhappy marriage? Now I'm almost hoping he doesn't take my advice!

Why did I ever come to work for a widower? I wish I'd live in a cute little house like Polly Mast, happy and carefree, planting flowers, tending my garden, and in the winter making quilts and reading books.

Oh, God, help Isaac to make the right decision! ✤

*I*saac has been uncommunicative, cool, and distant. I don't hold it against him. I know he's troubled, torn between his desire to follow my counsel, and his desire to follow his own heart.

Matthew's affectionate, loving baby ways have been a balm to my troubled soul. He's been trying to say "Miriam," and it comes out sounding more like "Mammy." That thrills my heart! It even drew a chuckle out of Isaac when he heard it.

Dear little Matthew! I only want happiness for you and your dad.

Today I sat at the sewing machine, making little shirts for Matthew and an apron for myself. The mornings are cool and frosty. I've been cleaning out the garden, carrying in pumpkins, and digging carrots. On the stove I have a drying pan of apples, which makes the whole kitchen smell good. Isaac loves dried apples, and even Matthew likes to chew on them.

This morning Isaac went out with the gun and brought

in a ring-necked pheasant. So now we'll have stuffed pheasant for supper.

If I wouldn't be so troubled about Isaac, I'd be perfectly happy. Is that the way it is for parents with children? They are a joy, yet their heartaches are your heartaches, their troubles your troubles.

Am I saying I feel like a mother to Isaac? No, I don't feel old enough to be his mother, but I'm sure I'm as concerned for his welfare and happiness as a mother would be. I love him in the way a mother would love her son.

This morning in my daily devotional I read: "Continual abiding in Christ is a life of exquisite and overflowing happiness." Doesn't that mean if I abide in Christ, troubles and cares won't make me unhappy because I know he will take care of them if I ask him? Doesn't it mean that all things will work together for good to those who love the Lord?

The devotional continues: "Such a life is a sacred thing. It gives a sanctity to every tone, act, and movement. There is a positive effectiveness that makes others feel that our bodies as well as our spirits are, indeed, the very temple of God. We are completely aware of God's presence within, constantly yielding every action and thought to his will. How would Jesus act? What would he say? Is this pleasing to God? It is praying without ceasing, communing with God continually."

It sounds wonderful indeed. I must live my life as Jesus would live it, and if I do that, I cannot live for myself.

Isaac's mother is no longer living. I will pray for Isaac as I know she would do if she'd be living. I like to think that God sent me here for a purpose. . . . 🌿

*T*oday was the wedding, Sally and Henry's. A wedding is a day of happiness and joy, feasting and celebration, and also a hallowed time, when two people step into holy matrimony together.

The spotlessly clean rooms were filled with chairs and benches. Tables in the cellar were loaded with prepared foods: cubed cheese, macaroni salad, dishes of pineapple tapioca, butterscotch pudding, chocolate cake, white cake, peaches, trays of cookies, jars of mixed candies.

In the summer kitchen the cooks were busy preparing the roast, mashed potatoes, gravy, filling, noodles, corn, and creamed celery.

I enjoyed listening to the wedding sermon. The chosen Scripture passages portrayed marriage and home life, and the preachers gave examples and instructions for harmonious living. Then came the exchanging of the wedding vows, testimonies, prayer, and closing hymn.

After the young people went upstairs, tables were set up to feed nearly four hundred people. The waitresses were busy carrying dishes of food up the cellar steps and empty dishes down again to be refilled. The cooks put the finishing touches on the hot foods and mashed the potatoes.

As the people were being seated at the tables, most had eyes only for the bride and groom, but I was looking for Isaac and Priscilla. I heard a peel of jolly laughter, and it wasn't hard to spot them then. After grace, Priscilla kept up lively talk with a man across the table, while Isaac sat quietly eating. At least it *sounded* like she was happy.

The day was over all too soon. Almost before I knew it, the time came to leave. Isaac took me with him; I didn't ask how Priscilla got home. On the way we stopped at Ben Esh's to pick up Matthew. Fifteen-year-old Ruth was doing the babysitting. She is a pretty, friendly girl, and so is her sister, Rosemary, who is twenty-one.

The first time I saw Rosemary, I thought, Now why couldn't Isaac have chosen a girl like her? Rosy cheeks, a sweet full mouth, sparkling eyes, heavy, dark-brown hair. Sincerity, friendliness, a worthy character, and faithfulness shine out of her eyes. But Priscilla's beauty seems to be only skin-deep, like it was painted on.

When I found out Rosemary was not dating anyone, I wondered even more. . . . ✼

*P*olly Mast had invited us to her house for a Christmas dinner. She roasted a stuffed turkey and had all the fixings to go with it. Ben Esh's were also there. Only today I found out that Mrs. Ben is Polly's sister. She's a kindhearted, motherly soul, and easy to visit with.

A cousin of Polly was there, too: Nate Mast, a bachelor in his forties, who actually lives not far from here. It's funny I never noticed him before. He's huskily built and has curly, almost-red hair, friendly crinkles around his eyes, and a ruddy face. I wonder why he hasn't married yet.

This afternoon I didn't have a boy. Rosemary and Ruth stole Matthew away from me, carried him off, and didn't return him until it was time to leave. Ben, Isaac, and Nate kept an interesting conversation going all afternoon. They sounded like old friends.

What a happy Christmas day this has been! I think of those who are hungry or out in the cold, friendless or sick. Lord, help me not to grow thoughtless or indifferent, but to give freely and to help wherever I am able. ✿

*W*inter has come. We awoke this morning to at least six inches of fresh, clean, dazzling country snow. I felt about as excited as a child. Last night Isaac had said that if it snows, we'll go to church on the sleigh.

I bundled up Matthew in a snowsuit and blanket and

myself in a coat and shawl, and we started out in the fresh wintry morning air. The sun came up, making the snow dazzle and sparkle, and we could see our breath in the frosty air.

The sermon was inspiring, and preachers Dan and Amos made it seem so real—the birth of Jesus in a humble stable, Mary and Joseph, the shepherds coming to worship the baby, the angels saying: "Peace on earth, good will toward men," the star that shone over the stable. The people that walked in the darkness have seen a great light. That light which enlightens every one was coming into the world. Because of Jesus' sacrificial life and death, that light is still shining.

On the way home we sang Christmas carols: "O Little Town of Bethlehem," "Joy to the World," "O Come All Ye Faithful." I haven't had so much fun for a long time.

Pretending

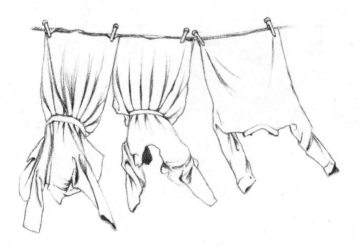

January 19

*T*he days are passing in swift succession. Isaac doesn't volunteer any information about his relationship with Priscilla, and I don't ask. He goes away Friday evenings and doesn't say where. He is himself again, jolly, talkative, given to teasing, and fun to be with.

Last week I had a different job for two days, caring for a new baby at Elam Raber's until their maid was able to come. I took Matthew along since Isaac was busy in the shop.

At the Raber's I bathed the baby, a girlie named Betsy, cared for the tots aged two and three, prepared the meals, and did the dishes and laundry. On Thursday Elam's sister Hannah Raber came to see the baby. She is an older single girl, perhaps in her late thirties. I've seen her at church and talked with her at times, but apparently she's not my kindred spirit, for no friendship blossomed between us.

Hannah is good looking, but it's not really a wholesome, vivacious beauty—more of a haunting, ethereal kind. When Isaac came to pick up Matthew and me to take us home, I asked him about Hannah. He told me that she and Nate Mast had been engaged a long time ago and had planned to be married. But then something happened—he didn't know what—and they parted and are both still single.

It's a strange, sad world. Life would be so meaningless if

we hadn't a loving heavenly Father to lead us and guide us in the way that he has planned for us. I will trust him, knowing that he makes no mistakes. 🌿

*O*h, I am terribly agitated and upset! I'll have to write down my feelings. How I wish Isaac would come home, and yet I dread to face him. About an hour ago a visitor came driving in the lane, tied his horse, and came to the door asking for Isaac.

I told him Isaac had gone to a sale, but he'd probably be home within a half hour. He waited about forty minutes, then came to the door again and said he couldn't wait any longer or it would be dark before he got home.

He acted nervous and kept clearing his throat. Finally he asked if I would give Isaac a message. I agreed, and for a few minutes he hemmed and hawed and then told me the bad news. He said he's a neighbor of Priscilla and that for a few weeks now a car has been stopping at Priscilla's place in the evening. She comes out of the house and climbs in, and the man drives away with her.

He said at first he thought nothing of it until just yesterday Bill Smith, the taximan, said that he saw Priscilla at the movies several times with a man and wondered what was going on. He felt it was his duty to say something to Isaac, and I'm glad he came by. But I wish so much Isaac would've been at home so I wouldn't have to be the one to tell him.

It seems like a bad dream. Isaac will come in, grab Matthew, and toss him up in the air. He'll cheerily ask, What's for supper? And then I'll have to drop the bomb. Oh God, give me the wisdom to break it gently, and give him the grace to bear it. 🌿

*T*here hasn't been much joy in this house the last month. Matthew and I had the flu, and with Isaac feeling so bad, laughter and smiles are about as rare as unicorns.

The entire church was shocked when they heard that Priscilla is now married to a divorced man. Poor girl! I feel so sorry for her. Now that there is no more danger of Isaac marrying Priscilla, my feelings toward her have turned to mostly pity. So young! So immature! I wish there would be some way I could help her.

I am positively alarmed and worried about Isaac. He walks around in a daze, not himself at all. I just wish there'd be some way I could get him to take some medication to tide him over this jolt.

Several times Isaac asked me, "Does God still love me?"

I tell him over and over, "God loves you very much, and the day will come when you will thank him that he didn't let you marry Priscilla. It's rough for you now, but at least you found out what she really is, before you married her."

Isaac dumbly shakes his head. He doesn't eat more than a few bites at mealtime, and at night I hear him pacing round in his room. I am literally praying without ceasing for him. Oh, what would we do without prayer, without our Burden Bearer? 🌿

*I*saac is feeling somewhat better and goes about his work like usual. Spring has returned at last. After that fateful day in February, it seemed like the winter lasted forever.

Now Isaac is preparing for spring planting, turning over the rich black earth, riding the sulky plow behind the horses. Daffodils, tulips, and hyacinths are blooming all over the place. Elizabeth must have loved flowers. Robins are sweetly singing, and new leaves are sprouting on the trees!

Yesterday I planted early peas, lettuce, cabbage, potatoes, carrots, onions, red beets, and parsley in the garden. How I love that job, putting the seeds in the ground and covering them! A gentle spring rain began to fall before I was quite finished. The robins seem to sing more joyously and sweetly when it rains.

Last week I took Matthew for the immunizations he was supposed to have at eighteen months of age. At the doctor's office I met Priscilla Kauf—oops, no longer Kauffman. At first she refused to look at me, but when everyone else had left the office, she came over and sat beside me.

She covered her face with her hands and said, "Oh Miriam, I've done such a dreadful thing. Oh, what shall I do?"

She cried heartbrokenly for a while. I prayed for help to know what to say. What could I say?

"Why did you do it?" I asked gently.

She cried some more, and it was a while before she could talk again. Then the words came tumbling out in a torrent.

"Oh, you wouldn't believe what kind of a man Dad is,"

she cried bitterly. "He left the church when I was five, and then he became the cruelest man that ever lived, and I hate him . . . hate him," she cried, clenching her fists.

She was so upset that I put my arm around the poor girl to comfort her as she sobbed.

"Dad abused and molested me for years," she murmured.

I gave her my handkerchief.

"I hate myself, and I hate all men. I can't stand being married," she moaned. "Oh, what shall I do? It seems the only time I'm happy is when I'm breaking some man's heart. Doing what I did to Isaac, deceiving him, and leading him on—that was worst of all."

She wept bitterly.

"Isaac is such a good, fine man."

At the beginning of her outburst, the doctor had opened the door from the inner office, and was quietly standing there, unknown to Priscilla. I looked helplessly at him.

"We'll take care of this," Dr. Wing said quietly. "We'll see that she gets counseling. Come into the office now, Priscilla."

Dr. Wing knows Isaac—he's been their family doctor for years, and also Priscilla's. I didn't realize that he understands Pennsylvania Dutch, though.

Poor Priscilla! She needs counseling, but she needs more than counseling. She needs Jesus to give her his forgiving grace, healing, and a new life.

I feel so sorry for Priscilla. How can I bear it? We hear of such things in the big cities, but they ought not to be out here in the country where the plain people are. Poor, poor girl!

How much should I tell Isaac? I think maybe I should let

him know everything. I want to do whatever I can for Priscilla. What can I possibly do besides visit her and pray for her? 🌿

*L*ast evening we had a thunder shower, and the freshly washed earth was sparkling in the sunshine this morning as we drove to church. The air smelled of flowers, woods, and fields. A blue bird flew to a post beside the road, and Matthew pointed to it and cried, "Mammie, look, birdie!" He calls me Mammie all the time now.

This was our communion Sunday, and how fitting that it should be held on Easter Sunday. Because Christ arose, we too are promised victory over sin and death as we follow him. How meaningful to partake of holy communion, the sign of Christ's body and blood, shed for the remission of sin! The service seemed to bind us together in obedience to our Master, the way of spiritual life and health.

Isaac is almost completely back to his old self now in his outward expression. He realizes that he was spared from even worse trouble, and he is grateful, although I know the inner wound will take more time to heal.

I wonder why some people can go through their entire life with their beloved marriage partner, while others, like Isaac, have to go through a double dose of pain and heartache. I guess we won't know until we reach the other side, that shining shore, where all tears will be wiped away, and then we'll understand why. 🌿

Sunday afternoon, while both Isaac and Matthew were napping, I went for a long walk, back through several fields, until I came to the most beautiful meadow I ever saw. The creek flowed through it, and the grass was lush and green and dotted with yellow buttercups. Bluebells bloomed in a hollow nearby. I was so astounded to have found such beauty that I flopped down on the grass, filled with gratitude and the joy of living, of being alive in such a place.

Soon I heard someone whistling nearby, and I jumped up quickly. What a surprise to see Nate Mast walking toward me! His hat was on at a rakish angle, and he was grinning as he called out, "Who's trespassing on my land?"

Nate came over and sat on the grass beside me. Right away I felt completely at ease with him.

"Is this really your land?" I asked.

"Yes, it's the back end of my farm. My buildings are over that rise," he said, waving his arm to show the direction.

We then talked of Isaac and Priscilla, and one thing led to another. He began talking about himself, how he and Hannah Raber had been engaged and were planning to be married. "But four weeks before the wedding date, she suddenly decided she didn't want to marry yet, after all."

I looked at him in sympathy. He was silent for a few moments, and his throat bulged as he struggled to swallow.

"I never cared for anyone else. A year later I asked her to reconsider, but she was still sure she wasn't ready to get married. I asked her several more times, and always the answer was no. When Mother died, I asked her again, with the same result."

"What's wrong with her?" I blurted out.

Then I realized how that sounded and started to laugh. Nate laughed, too, and wiped away a tear.

I realized that he still cares deeply and is still hurting. Suddenly I was struck by what I thought was a brilliant idea. Impulsively, without thinking, I said, "You know what you ought to do?"

"No. What?"

"You ought to pretend you're getting interested in another woman. That would probably bring her around faster than anything else would."

He stared at me for a few minutes, then exclaimed, "Hey, I believe you really have something there! Why didn't I ever think of that? I just might try it."

Suddenly I realized it was high time to hike myself home and jumped up and bade him farewell.

I had a lot to think about on the way back. Nate is a nice chap, and I think he deserves happiness. But I hope he doesn't marry Hannah. Somehow I feel sure the two are not suited together at all.

Tonight when Isaac and I went for our evening drive with Matthew, I told him about my chance meeting with Nate.

"Isn't it strange?" I said. "Most men would've married someone else. There are other fish in the sea, as they say. Why do you think he didn't?"

"Maybe it was God's will," Isaac answered. And then, teasingly, "Maybe he's reserved for you."

I felt like poking him in the ribs. If it would be proper for a housekeeper to poke a widower, I would've done so with relish. Instead, I pretended I hadn't heard by saying, "He still cares deeply about Hannah and still wants her.

"Well," Isaac said, "it's his life. His dad didn't get married until he was forty-four, and he had six children yet. Perhaps Nate will, too." 🌿

May 17

*M*ay is such a lovely month. Ah . . . the blossoming fruit trees! There's a pear tree outside the kitchen window, and those fragrant blossoms floating down are like a foretaste of heavenly splendor.

I'm sitting on the vine-shaded porch, watching a butterfly flitting around in my garden. I think there's almost nothing nicer than a garden in May: The neat rows of peas and potatoes, the other early vegetables, and bright colorful petunias bordering it.

Just now Matthew brought me a pink petunia. I praised and thanked him and gave him a hug. Whenever I think that sometime we must be parted, my throat tightens, almost as if a lump would be forming.

I want Isaac to be happy. Never would I have wished him the heartache that Priscilla caused. And yet I'm glad I can stay a while longer. Secretly, I'm hoping he'll fall in love with Rosemary Esh. Perhaps I'll invite her and her family over for a meal sometime—or would that be too obvious?

Today at church, the text really struck me: Be ye therefore followers of God, as dear children; and walk in love, as Christ also has loved us, and has given himself for us an offering and a sacrifice to God for a sweet-smelling savor.

How do we walk in love? One of the fruits of the Spirit is love. If we have God's Spirit within, can we love even those who mistreat us or despitefully use us? Can we judge and interpret kindly and pray for such people, returning good for evil? Can we refrain from unkind gossip? With God, all things are possible.

I've been thinking a lot about Priscilla and wishing I could visit her. The church took counsel together and decided they had to excommunicate her for marrying a divorced man. I know Preachers Amos and Dan visited her several times and expressed their concern and care. But maybe she needs someone who is closer to her, someone to confide in. 🌿

June 1

I really have gotten myself into something. On Sunday evening Isaac, Matthew, and I were sitting on lawn chairs under the willow tree, talking of going for a drive. Then who should come driving in the lane but Nate Mast!

Isaac called to him, "Come and join the party."

"I thought Miriam might go for a drive with me."

A few minutes later I found myself sitting beside Nate in his carriage behind his big sorrel horse trotting out the lane. We talked of the nice evening, the weather last week, and the crops. Finally he cleared his throat several times and got up enough courage to tell me what was on his mind. Nate wants me to "go with him" a few evenings to see if we can get Hannah jealous enough to take him back, as I had suggested the other Sunday.

I don't know whether to laugh or cry! I believe I am in shock. Anyhow, we drove past Hannah's place, and she was sitting on a blanket in the front yard. I waved, but she just looked and looked and looked.

After we were past, I couldn't help but laugh. The more I tried to stop, the harder I laughed, and Nate had to laugh, too. I think we both felt more like a pair of teenagers than over forty. We turned around after a mile or so and passed her place again on the way back, but she wasn't in the yard anymore and neither was the blanket.

On the way home Nate asked me not to tell anyone about our scheme. Such a juicy morsel of gossip would be sure to fly, and if Hannah found it out, the plan wouldn't work.

I told him I would have to tell Isaac, but he said he'd rather I didn't. That will be hard. I don't want Isaac to think that Nate and I are dating. Oh well, it probably won't be long until Hannah changes her mind. . . . ✿

June 12

*T*hese last few weeks have been busy with peas and strawberries. This afternoon I made a luscious strawberry pie topped with whipped cream, and now I can hardly wait to surprise Isaac.

He's busy with the hay, and if I wouldn't be so busy myself, I'd love to help, too. There is a warm, fragrant south wind blowing over the new-mown hay fields, and the sweet fragrance of the rambler roses on the trellis floats in through the open kitchen window. "What is so rare as a day in June?" (J. R. Lowell).

Yesterday afternoon Polly Mast came to help with the strawberries. The first thing she said when she came in the door was "Congratulations!" I must have had a blank look on my face, for she added, "To you and Nate."

What could I say? I merely smiled and tactfully changed the subject. She must not know the secret!

It was such a pleasure to chat with her once again. I don't get over to visit her as often as I'd like. Polly has such forthright opinions about people and things. I think I'll adopt her for the sister I never had. Matthew likes her, too. She likes children and has a way with them.

Isaac is in for supper, so I must go. 🌿

June 16

We were invited to Ben Esh's for supper tonight. I was glad because it would be an excellent opportunity for Isaac to notice Rosemary, I thought. Hmmm, no other guests! A delicious supper. Wonderful fellowship. They are dear, good people.

Then, surprise of surprises, Rosemary carried in a big, beautifully decorated birthday cake with candles. Everyone sang, "Happy birthday to you, Happy birthday to you, Happy birthday, dear Miriam, Happy birthday to you!"

I was simply struck dumb. Matthew clapped his hands and laughed gleefully and said, "Mammie, cakie."

Everyone burst out laughing at that.

"How did you know?" I finally managed to ask. "I never told a single soul it's my birthday."

Rosemary blushed and said, "A little bird told me."

"Who was the little bird?" I asked innocently.

She glanced at Isaac, and then I saw him blushing, too.

What's going on between those two behind my back?

There's something happening, I'm sure. I quizzed Isaac about it on the way home, and he was ready with a comeback: "You don't expect me to sit at home alone when you go for drives with Nate, do you?"

"I understand now!" I responded as I thought, "God's in his heaven—All's right with the world" (R. Browning). What a good excuse my birthday gave Rosemary to invite Isaac over! 🍃

June 22

*L*ast evening Isaac took Matthew and left to see Rosemary, and I was dolefully wondering if I'd have to spend the Sunday evening alone. Then I spied Nate's dear old sorrel horse trotting in the lane. Instantly discouragement and weariness dropped from my spirit, and I jumped up to get ready. Instead of turning around and waiting for me to climb in like he usually does, he drove to the railing and tied the horse.

"How about a walk to the back meadow?" he asked.

"Yes, let's," I responded eagerly.

It's the most beautiful place I ever saw. We strolled along the old cow lane, the birds were twittering in the bordering trees, and it was a lovely evening.

Walking beside Nate gave me a queer little thrill, and I thought, Careful there, old girl, you must not let your heart get involved. Remember, this is all for show, to woo another lady.

Then it dawned on me: This won't do anything to make Hannah jealous if she doesn't know anything about it. I told Nate so.

"Tut, tut," he said briskly. "Maybe in a roundabout way."

I found some wild rose bushes, and Nate pulled out his pocket knife to cut a bouquet of lovely pink blossoms for me. He told me teasingly that I ought to put them in my hair. It was such a sweet, pleasant evening.

Nate has a boat on the creek back there, and we went for a ride. The calm stillness of the water was broken only by an occasional splash of an oar. Being with him seems so right. I feel so relaxed around him. There is often no need to talk, just a companionable silence between us.

We're both nature lovers, and we enjoy watching the flickering fireflies, gazing at a big full moon rising over the horizon, feeling the caressing breeze frolicking and dancing among the leaves—these are things of awesome wonder to us both.

Presently Nate began to talk, first about experiences of the past, then about the yet-untrodden future, full of hopes and dreams and wonderful possibilities. I wonder if Hannah will share that future with him.

Time goes so fast when I'm with him, and it was late when we got back. Isaac was already at home and sitting at the kitchen table when I walked in.

"So, how goes the courting?" he teased. "It must be great, as late as it is."

I blushed—now why did I do that?—and reversed the question to him.

"Great!" was his answer.

I'm so happy for him. He deserves happiness if anyone does. 🌿

July 10

*T*he summer days are slipping away, filled with work and dreams, joys, and sometimes sadness. I am in the midst of potty training Matthew. I expect it may take me several months, and I'd like to be sure it's finished before he gets a new Mammy.

Isaac brought in an armload of sweet corn today, and the tomatoes will soon be ripe. We're already eating new potatoes, and I can hardly wait until the lima beans are ready. Such delicious garden goodies, abundant blessings! May we not forget to thank the Giver.

Well, Nate's plan is working, and I'm not sure whether I'm sad or glad. Yesterday I got a letter in the mail with no return address on it. Inside was a single sheet, with no greeting, no "Dear Miriam," no signature—just three short sentences: "Please stay away from Nate Mast. He does not belong to you. He is promised to another." That was all!

Why is a tear slipping down my cheek? I guess if I want to admit it, I *am* sad. I enjoy being with Nate immensely. On Sunday he took me over to see his place. I fell in love with it immediately. So quaint and old-fashioned!

The creek makes a turn right behind the house, and it runs a creaking waterwheel that Nate has rigged with a cable to pump his water. The house is surrounded by trees, and there's a springhouse at the side. In front there's a windmill with phlox growing around it.

The farmhouse is in good repair and surprisingly clean for a bachelor. He told me that his mother died last year, and I figured out that it was just one month before *my* mother died. Since then, one of his nieces comes once a week to help with the household chores.

"It's a lonely life," he said, and added, "What's a home without a woman's heart and a child's presence?"

I was strangely stirred by those words. He looked so vulnerable and sad as he said them, and I almost felt as if I should reach out and comfort him.

Now the letter! There is no doubt in my mind that Hannah wrote it. I must show it to Nate. ✽

July 21

    *T*he community has been shocked and saddened this week. Allen Keim's wife, Frieda, has been diagnosed as having leukemia, the fast-going kind. I spent the afternoon at Polly's place, and she told me about it.

Allen is taking it quite hard. They have a family of seven children, the oldest being twenty years old and the youngest three. She is a rare jewel of a wife, according to Polly, and she doubts whether anyone would be good enough to take her place. No wonder it's so hard on Allen!

The day before yesterday was our in-between (alternate) Sunday, when we didn't have church. At Nate's suggestion, I packed a picnic lunch, and Isaac, Rosemary, and Matthew, and Nate and I picnicked beside Nate's beloved creek. We all drove over on the spring wagon. It was a beautiful day. The fields and meadows shimmered in the light of the July afternoon, and a light wind danced over the water and through the leaves.

By the creek it was cool, shady, and delightful. We sat and talked until after the food was all gone. Matthew had great fun throwing stones and sticks into the water. Presently Isaac and Rosemary sauntered off, and finally I had a chance to show Nate the letter.

I thought he'd probably throw back his head and laugh, delighted that the plan was working. Instead, he only frowned and stuffed the letter into his pocket. There was something about the outline of his lips that told me he wasn't pleased.

He suggested, "Let's forget about it for today." Then he talked of something else.

"Isn't this a beautiful, interesting world?" I commented. "It's easy to be happy on a day like this."

"Are you happy when you're with me?" he asked shyly.

"Oh yes!" I exclaimed. "I like it so much being out here by the creek."

He looked as if he were about to say something else, but then changed his mind.

The truth is, the time I spend with Nate is incredibly dear and precious. ✿

*O*h, for a breath of fresh air. I am sitting here fanning myself. I just took four crusty golden loaves of bread out of the oven, and now a delicious aroma fills the kitchen.

Yesterday Polly and I took her horse and drove the twelve miles to visit Priscilla. Her man left her last week, and now she's staying with her aunt and uncle. I felt so sorry for her, and I hope she'll let God untangle the tragic affairs of her life.

"Oh, what a tangled web we weave, When first we practice to deceive!" (W. Scott). When I thought of the fate dealt to her by her dad, I wanted to hold her and stroke her hair and comfort her. Poor child! ✿

*M*atthew's second birthday! He received a birthday card from his grandmother, and he was so pleased that he carried it around most of the day. I made him a birthday cake with lighted candles. Watching his face, shining eyes, and delighted smile—almost made me wish for a camera. Will I ever forget how he looked as he blew out the candles one by one?

Tonight Isaac hitched up one of his horses, and we went for a drive once again. It seemed like old times when neither Nate nor Rosemary had yet entered the picture.

It was so nice and peaceful, dusk settling over the land and the night insects chirping. The cool evening air felt so comfortably delicious.

Thank you, Father, for all our wondrous blessings. 🌿

August 6

*T*oday Rosemary spent the day here helping to do lima beans and can apple sauce. She's a joy to work with, energetic, and cheerful. I am inspired by the way her whole face lights up when she smiles.

Isaac will be all right with her, and Matthew too. He likes her already. She will bring sweet joy and happiness to this household, and fill it with the priceless joy of love.

I try not to think of my future. Where will I go and what will I do? I'm praying for God to give me a place to work where I can be a channel for his love, to make this a pleasanter world for others, to bring someone happiness or help in the Christian life.

Oh, how will I be able to bear it when Nate and Hannah are published to be married? How could I attend the wedding? So utterly foolish I was to think that my heart would not become involved!

Tears and heartache will be my portion. But I shall show a cheerful face, and nary a soul shall ever know that I've fallen in love with Nate! 🌿

*I*t's hard to believe a year has passed since I arrived here. Then Matthew was a baby; now he's an active toddler starting to talk in short sentences. It was so sweet to be a Mammy for a year!

On Sunday evening Nate and I went boating in the twilight. The bullfrogs were croaking their poignant, thrilling, melancholy songs, and I felt a twinge of sadness, a premonition that our so-called romance will soon be coming to an end.

Nate must have felt the same way because he said, "This has been such a happy summer. I feel as if I don't want it to end. The times I spent with you have been among the happiest of my life."

"I feel the same way," I responded. Then, feeling perhaps we were getting into dangerous waters—in conversation, not in boating!—I quickly changed the subject.

Lightning was flashing occasionally in the sky and thunder rumbling in the distance. When there was an abrupt, louder clap of thunder, Nate asked, "Are you getting frightened?"

"No," I replied, "I'm never frightened when I'm with you."

"In that case," he said, "since you're trusting me to take care of you, I'm taking you to the house right now. It sounds like it's coming fast."

By the time we pulled up the boat, it was sprinkling. So we ran to the house. Laughing and out of breath, we made it inside just as a heavy downpour began.

Nate made coffee, got out a tin of cookies, and brought out a box of beautiful, perfectly shaped arrowheads. Collecting them is one of his hobbies, and so is hunting and fishing. Above his desk hang several calendars showing wilderness scenes, and on his desk are a stack of old magazines about hunting and fishing. I suppose those hobbies somewhat took the place of a wife and children for him. But not much longer will they do that!

September 1

*T*oday was the funeral of Frieda Keim. I'll never forget that scene as the sorrowing family stood around the casket for the last time, with bowed heads and shaking with sobs. The oldest girl is twelve years old, and she seemed to be taking it the hardest. Their dear, precious mother being lowered into the ground! How can they bear it?

Death is so final, so cruel, so hard to bear. Oh God, be with the family. Show me what I can do to help them.

Frieda's mother, a widow, has been living with them since Frieda was ill and will stay indefinitely.

In order to alleviate the pain in my heart as I watched the pitiful scene, I imagined what it must be like in the heavenly portals above: Frieda arriving there and being welcomed in, being given a robe of righteousness to wear, rejoicing to be with Jesus—wondrous joy and gladness!

And then I also envisioned the entire family being reunited someday in heaven. Allen and Frieda being together again, and all the children with them, never to be parted again, never to sorrow or suffer again, only eternal joy and gladness and life with God.

May we all strive to be ready when our call comes. 🌿

*I*t's silo-filling time—a season of year I love. It gives us a sense of space and openness to have the fields cleared once again. We're enjoying the cooler weather returning, crisp cool mornings, mellow sunshine, the sweet scent of grapes ripening on the vines, apples to pick. It's back to school for the children and teachers. Soon the trees will hang out bright, colorful leaves.

Matthew is playing on the floor with his blocks. He's out of diapers, picks up his toys, and follows instructions. I'm thinking how fortunate I am to have such a good, sweet boy like him in my care. The things I've read about temper tantrums, terrible twos, spanking, and battles of wills—these aren't a problem with him.

Already there are leaves to rake in the front yard, and I trimmed and mowed all around the house again today. It hadn't been necessary last week, but now it looks so much better again. What smells better than freshly mowed grass?

The flowers have put on a burst of fresh, showy bloom, almost as if they know their time is short and that Jack Frost will soon claim them. There are colorful zinnias, bright yellow marigolds, pink and red geraniums, blue ageratums, and red firebranch.

Last week another unsigned letter came—a disturbing reminder for me to stay in my place, and a question about my purpose for being with Nate. I know I've lost my heart hopelessly to him, but nobody shall ever know but you, dear diary. On our drives and hikes we have long talks about our hopes, dreams, and ideals.

I enjoy talking with Isaac, too, but he is so much younger, and also I have more in common with Nate. Why is it so easy and natural for me to discuss my innermost feelings with him? Maybe because of our triangle relationship.

If Nate would be my beau, coming to court me, perhaps I'd feel more reserved and self-conscious, more like I should always be putting my best foot forward. But with him in this pretend courtship, I can be myself and nobody cares. ❧

October 4

*T*onight after Matthew had been put to bed, Isaac asked, "Care to join me on the porch swing for awhile?"

"Sure," I consented readily. "It's been a while since we've had a real talk. We've been too busy to take any evening drives lately."

The evening was warm and balmy, a summerlike south breeze blowing, and the moon rising up over the horizon. Crickets were chirping, and there was an aura of sweet peace and serenity in the dusky twilight.

We talked awhile of other things, and then he told me of his wedding plans. He and Rosemary are being married on Thanksgiving Day. I'm so happy for them. Yet what will I do then? Where will I go?

However, my mind had to snap back to the present. Isaac was still talking: "Would you and Nate like to have a double wedding with us? Rosemary said she would be happy to do it that way if you want to."

For a few moments I just sat there, stunned! Then I quickly jumped up and exclaimed, "Oh no, that wouldn't suit us at all!" And I ran into the house.

Poor Isaac! I guess he didn't know what came over me. For the first time I fully realized—it really dawned on me that we are deceiving people, actually living a lie. Oh, I'm so ashamed! My face feels so hot. Now I cannot go on with the plan. I must tell Nate that it's over.

Why am I crying? O God, forgive me and help me. 🌿

October 20

Today all the women of the district came together to houseclean at Allen Keim's. Many hands make light work and chores more fun. We cleaned and scrubbed the house from top to bottom, and we raked and cleaned the yard. The children are fortunate to have their grandmother there. She is a good, kind soul.

After the work was finished and some women had left already, Hannah came over to me. "I'd like to have a talk with you before we leave."

"Let's go upstairs and look at the freshly cleaned rooms," I responded. "Everything is now in place, and there we'll have some privacy."

She slumped down on a bed and began to admonish me, "Miriam, I wish you'd stay away from Nate. I think it's rude and bold of you to butt in like this when you know I don't like it."

I lost my cool. Without thinking, I gave her some straight talk: "You don't want him. He's wanted you for years already, and you rejected him every time. What claim do you have on him? What right do you have to warn me away?"

"I know, that's right," she murmured, then continued with more strength: "But now I've changed my mind. I'm ready to marry him, and I'm sorry I put him off. Will you tell him to come, see me on Sunday?"

"Me tell him!" I sputtered. "I wouldn't have the chance. After all, he's coming to see *me* on Sunday evening," I finished lamely.

"Well, then tell him then to come, see me on Monday," she insisted as she walked primly out the door.

The nerve of her! The very nerve! She must feel like she has the right to control everyone and everything! I waited until I was at home to have a good cry, and then I shed tears of frustration and disappointment. I am angry at myself for being such a goose.

A few weeks ago I had resolved to tell Nate that I would no longer take part in his scheme, that it's wrong and living a lie. But that Sunday I thought, Just this one time yet won't matter. And when I tried to get up enough willpower to tell him, it all fell away.

I'm just a weak, sinful mortal, a self-righteous prig. Isaac thinks I am a good Christian, but I'm nothing of the sort. How weak-willed and selfish I am! I eat when I'm hungry, and I drink when I'm dry. I want *what* I want and *when* I want it.

What's more, lately I've been neglecting my prayer life, and I haven't felt close to God. What did Preacher Dan say about doing nothing that cools our love for the heavenly bridegroom? I've backslidden, I've grieved the Holy Spirit of God!

Oh God, forgive me. . . . Now I'm ready to surrender my life into your hands again, instead of taking my own selfish way. Have mercy upon me, O God, according to your loving-kindness: according to the multitude of your tender mercies, blot out my transgressions. Wash me thoroughly from my iniquity, and cleanse me from my sin.

I just finished having a heartrending, soul-wrenching cry, and now I feel drained and at peace.

October 26

*S*unday was one of those calm, golden autumn days, mild, and balmy. In the evening Nate drove in, and I walked out to his carriage, fully intending not to get in. I would just tell him what Hannah said and that our relationship was over.

But he called out jovially, "Jump in! We're going for the last boat ride of the season."

Before I knew what was happening, we were driving out the lane at a fast clip, and Nate and I were talking away, just like old times.

Sitting in the boat, floating gently with the current, leaves whirling down into the water—I cleared my throat to tell Nate.

Just then he began speaking. "Miriam, do you realize how much you mean to me?"

I shook my head and opened my mouth to tell him what I must, but he was still talking: "The memory of your smile is like a benediction to me. When I have to make a decision, I think, What would Miriam do? You help me to choose the good and right way."

"That's nice," I responded, and quickly added, "I had a talk with Hannah last week."

He waved a hand and declared, "Let's forget about Hannah for a while. It's us I want to talk about."

"But Hannah said she wants to marry you now," I quickly put in.

That stunned him completely. He sat there speechless.

"So, I'll be going," I added as I rowed for the shore. I stood up to jump off.

"Wait, Miriam," Nate cried, and grabbed my hand.

I jerked my hand away and jumped, stepping into water up to my knees in my haste to get the bank. Without saying good-bye, I fled homeward, crying and stumbling through the fields.

I was so glad Isaac wasn't home yet. I wouldn't have wanted him to see my face. To the solace of my room I went, to cry and cry and cry. . . .

Now the stormy tempest of tears is over, and I am at peace because I feel I've done the right thing. The future is unknown, but Jesus is with me, and he will lead me and guide me.

But, oh dear, I forgot to tell Nate to see Hannah on Monday! I guess she'll just have to deliver her own message. 🍃

November 5

*I*saac is happily excited about the plans for his wedding, and I am rejoicing with him. But my own life seems stale and flat just now. In all probability, it's the letdown after my summer romance.

Underneath is the big question, What next? Polly has invited me to come and live with her, and it sure is tempting, but I haven't received any clear guidance yet. I should be finishing the housecleaning. Everything must be sparkling clean and shipshape before Rosemary steps in—but I haven't much heart for any kind of work, nor much of an appetite, either.

On Wednesday morning last week, I told Isaac that it was all over between Nate and me and that there never really was anything between us. He looked at me in a puzzled way, and I don't think he was fooled for a minute. Nevertheless, I am determined that no one, but no one, shall know of the pain and heartache in my bosom.

That is, no one but my Friend and Savior, Jesus Christ, the Burden Bearer, who will carry me, as well as my burden, if I let him. Oh, precious thought! How sweet my fellowship with him has been since I've surrendered all to him again. I am hoping for some work through which I can forget self and the afflictions of my own heart, in Christ's service. In other words, I want to lose myself in service for the Master.

From my devotional book: "By nature, the heart is full of selfishness. Even the believer's own salvation and happiness are too often one's only object. But by abiding in Jesus, we come into contact with his infinite love. That fire of love begins to burn within our heart, we see the beauty of love, and we learn to look upon loving and serving our fellows as the highest privilege a disciple of Jesus can have."

Today I got a letter from friend Mary. Thank God for good, kind friends. She sent a little poem which I will copy here.

Oh, the Cross has wondrous glory!
    Oft I've proved this to be true;
When I'm in the way so narrow,

I can see a pathway through;
And how sweetly Jesus whispers:
 "Take the Cross, thou need'st not fear,
For I've tried the way before thee,
 And the glory lingers near." (Anon.)

I wonder if Mary knows how I feel. As I look back over my life, I see much sin and selfishness, murmuring and self-serving. Oh God, forgive me! May the rest of my life be one of unselfish service for you, daily dying to self and its demands. ✿

November 16

*E*lizabeth's mother, Anna Beiler, is here for an extended visit. She wants to become reacquainted with her grandson, Matthew, and to attend the wedding next week. Anna helped finish the cleaning and cheered my weary heart. We baked cookies and pies and caught up with the sewing.

I think God sent her at just the right time. She was just what I needed to help me snap out of my melancholy. Evenings we sit and talk until late. If Elizabeth was like her mother, it's no wonder Isaac loved her. Matthew adores his grandma, and she holds him and shows him picture books whenever he asks her to.

Our prayers for Isaac have been answered. When I think to last March when I was worried about his emotional health, I thank God for his mercy and loving-kindness. Now I'd like to ask Isaac, Do you think God loved you when he prevented you from marrying Priscilla? But, I wouldn't do that.

I had often wondered how Isaac ever started to get interested in Priscilla. Now today Anna said that when her daughter Rebecca was working here, she had been a friend to Priscilla, and Priscilla often came to visit. I wonder if that was her intention in the first place, to capture Isaac's heart.

Anna told me, too, that at that time Rosemary was dating someone else. Too bad! Maybe if she had been free, Isaac would have been spared the heartache he had with Priscilla. Yet now we can say, "All is well that ends well" (J. Heywood). 🍃

November 25

*T*his afternoon we all went over to Ben Esh's to help get ready for the wedding. Isaac raked leaves, I helped clean the kitchen, and Anna helped cook the cornstarch pudding. That was fun! I really enjoyed being there. A wedding truly is a time of rejoicing.

There's a rosy sunset in the west tonight, and it looks for a sunny day tomorrow.

Now for the important news: This afternoon I was up on a ladder washing windows outside when who should come around the corner of the house but Allen Keim, and he wanted to talk with me. He's a quiet, soft-spoken, unassuming man of medium build and height, and he had a little boy of about five years old along.

He greeted me formally, made some polite small talk, and then asked, "Do you have plans all made for when you're through working for Isaac?"

"No, I don't. I really don't know what I'll do."

"Well, then would you consider working for us? My mother-in-law is with us now, but it's too much for her. She has a bad heart."

"Oh really?" I said sympathetically. "I always thought it was so nice for the children to have their grandmother with them."

"Yes, it sure is. But the doctor told her last week she's not supposed to do any work."

"Could I think it over and give you my answer tomorrow at the wedding?" I asked.

"Sure thing. You do that." With those words, he left.

My thoughts were churning. That would certainly be a lot of responsibility. Being a substitute mother, training and disciplining and running the household. I don't feel capable of it. What should I say? I'm praying for clear guidance from the Lord.

If I'd follow my heart, I'd say, Oh no, please no, I don't want to work for another widower. I can't and I won't!

But I know if God wants me to go, he'll help me and strengthen me and give me the necessary wisdom. ❦

November 26, Thanksgiving

*I*saac and Rosemary's wedding! The day dawned clear, bright, and sunny, and we left early in order to be the first ones there. Matthew looked so adorably sweet in his new little suit, and Isaac looked handsomer than ever. He can't conceal his happiness, and no wonder. Such a rare jewel of a wife he's getting, and he deserves her, too.

Today I was a guest of honor—no cooking or dishwashing for me. After the inspiring sermon, Isaac and Rosemary stood and were asked the necessary questions. They exchanged their vows. We knelt for prayer, and then sang the wedding hymns.

Everything went as planned, neatly and orderly. A delicious meal was served, and the afternoon was spent visiting and singing. I had a chance to talk to Allen and told him I would be willing to take the job, under the condition that Frieda's mother will stay, even though she won't be able to do any work. She could still be a mother-figure to the children, give counsel and advice, help to plan and manage the work, and hold things together.

Allen said he would find out whether she would stay and let me know soon.

Oh, why did I say I would do it? I'm tired, and I shrink from the responsibility of stepping into a home like that. Besides, I'm longing for a home of my own. I have to think of the song: "My Ways, My Child, Are Not Your Ways, My Thoughts Are Higher Than Thine."

Neither Nate nor Hannah were at the wedding. Why do I keep thinking about them? I'd like to put them completely out of my mind. When the burdens are so heavy and I almost fall, I realize I'm trying to carry them myself again. I must give them all to Jesus, and then I'll have sweet peace, trusting him to lead me in his perfect will.

"Trust in the Lord with all your heart. . . . In all your ways acknowledge him, and he shall direct your paths." 🍃

*T*he day after the wedding Allen came for me, and Isaac and Rosemary came home. Another chapter of my life is ended.

It will take a while to adjust to life here at Allen's. I'm so glad I required Grandma (as everyone calls her) to stay. I don't believe I'd last long here if it wouldn't be for her. She's only in her sixties, but her heart is worn out and she must sit in her rocker all day.

What a shock that must have been for Grandma to get the news! Apparently she thought she was in fairly good health until just a few weeks ago she had a blackout spell. She was hospitalized for a few days for extensive testing and then received the verdict. But she's so cheerful and happy, and she radiates joy to all.

The three big boys, Clyde, Noah, and Eli—aged twenty, eighteen, and fiteen—are friendly, respectful, and helpful. Twelve-year-old Rachel is another story. She's openly resentful and hostile toward me, and I don't know why. Poor girl, having to lose her precious mother! I hope to win her over with love and God's help.

The little boys, Dave and Abram, nine and five, are mischievous but lovable. Then the baby of the family, three-year-old Mary, has blue eyes and blonde hair and is everyone's pet. I fear that she'll be spoiled if we aren't careful. She's so adorable and lovable.

Allen is still grieving deeply and noticeably. Grandma told me that he has not been himself since the funeral. He needs prayers and encouragement.

We're in a different district here, and today at church I met new faces and missed the old. I even missed Mamie

Lapp. Mary sat with me at church. Since Matthew always went with Isaac, it's the first time I ever took "a little person" along, and it gave me a queer thrill of happiness.

It's time to do the evening milking of the cows. The one cow is somewhat of a kicker for me. I guess she knows I'm afraid of her and takes advantage of it. The boys have their other chores, and last evening I had a battle with her while Allen was working nearby. I called to him, and he came and quieted her for me.

Allen said he's ashamed to be such a coward that he makes me do the milking, but he can't bear to do it himself. He shared that he and Frieda used to do the milking together, one on each side of the same cow. That was their time to talk, a precious time of togetherness. He brushed away a tear as he said it. Now he can't bear the thought of doing the milking without her.

Poor man! I can't fully realize the pain he's going through. All I can do is pray for him.

And I will be brave and milk that cow! 🍃

*O*h, what will I do about Rachel? This afternoon I was butchering chickens. Grandma, on the way to her room to take her nap, told Rachel to help me. The boys beheaded, defeathered, and singed the chickens, and then brought them in. I gave Rachel a bright smile and asked her if she'd ever helped butcher chickens before.

She must have decided it was not necessary to answer. I got a dishpan of water ready and washed the first chicken, then told her to wash the second one just like I'd done.

"No," she retorted. "You're not my boss."

That got my dander up, and I wondered if she was too big to spank. But that would not have been the right course in this case, even though I felt like it.

I asked Rachel if she'd rather cut off the chicken's legs.

Still no answer.

Mary had climbed up on the counter to watch, and I decided that for a time I'd just ignore Rachel. I chatted with Mary and answered her questions and told her a story as I worked.

Rachel sat on the sofa and read the *Family Life* magazine. She would never dare do that in Grandma's presence when she was supposed to be working. The minute she heard her footsteps coming out of her bedroom, she jumped up and grabbed a knife and pretended to help.

I tried to be as friendly and helpful as possible, and with Grandma in the kitchen it went a lot better. I wish I'd know how I could help Rachel. Last evening as I passed the door to her room, I heard her crying softly. Perhaps she sees me as taking the place of her mother, and that's why she resents me so. I'm praying without ceasing for wisdom to know how to handle her. 🍃

December 16

I'm finding it hard to get used to cooking here. Grandma has some decided opinions on what one should eat and what to avoid. Her theory is that you should use everything as nearly as possible in the way God gave it to us. Milk is all right, but not butter. "God never meant for us to separate the cream from the rest of the milk and make butter," she says. "That's why it's unhealthy."

The same with sugar. To her, it's something that's very unhealthy. She says it would be all right if we'd eat the whole sugar beet, fiber and all, the way God made it. But to refine the sugar out and add it to food, that's unhealthy, not God's will. And the flours—they're all right if from whole grain, but absolutely not if milled and the wheat germ and outer husk removed. . . . Therefore, white flour is a no-no.

Cheese is out for the same reason as butter. Whenever possible, vegetables and fruits should be eaten with the skins on—such as potatoes and apples. Rice is fine, but not polished white rice—only brown rice. Bread, crackers, and pretzels made from white flour should not be used.

I wonder how she arrived at these theories. I'm sure it's all right for her, with her heart trouble, but should she force this mode of eating on Allen and the children?

Yesterday Allen went to the grocery store and bought a bag of sugar and a bag of white flour. He carried them in with the other groceries, and before he went out the door, he said in a low voice so Grandma wouldn't hear, "Make some apple pies this afternoon."

So I was put on the spot. I knew that to be in the good graces of Grandma, I should not make the pies. But Allen had told me to, and since he's paying me to work for him, I decided I would have to make the pies. So I rolled up my sleeves, got out the rolling pin and supplies, and began.

Fortunately, Grandma went to her room for her nap. When she came out, the kitchen was filled with the wonderful aroma of freshly baked apple pies. She walked over to inspect them. I had prepared myself to see her pinching her mouth shut and sulking the rest of the day, or giving me a scolding.

But Grandma wouldn't do that. She smiled and said, "My, these pies smell good. You did the right thing in making them when Allen asked you to."

So she *had* heard!

"I suppose everyone has to learn the hard way," she added sadly, "like I did."

At suppertime when I carried a pie to the table, I was greeted by cheers from the family, and two whole pies disappeared fast. 🌿

*W*e had visitors this afternoon. I'm thinking back to the happy Christmas I had last year. This year it's different. There's the trouble with Rachel. She seems to be more resentful than ever, and there's no sign of change for the better.

Also, Allen has taken a turn for the worse, perhaps because of the memory of other joyous Christmas days when Frieda was still here. And worst of all, the doctor was here to see Grandma last week, and when he walked through the kitchen to leave, he stopped to have a little talk with me.

"With her heart in the shape it is, she could go at any time," he declared solemnly.

That agitated me greatly. Maybe it wasn't the right thing to do after all, to ask her to stay. Should the children be subjected to another death in the family? It doesn't seem right. I am disturbed about it.

Grandma never complains, and she is so serene and at peace. I think I should talk it over with her. Allen is in no shape to make a decision just now. I feel so sorry for him. He's miserable, and his nerves aren't in the best shape. Oh, what would I do if I'd have to carry these burdens alone?

Oh God, show me what I can and should do to help these people I'm working for. Give me guidance and wisdom to do and say the right thing. If it's your will, spare Grandma while she's so badly needed here. Heal the pain and grief in Allen's heart, restore his soul, and give him peace and joy in you. ✽

Substitute Mother

January 1

*N*ew Year's Day is a time of new beginnings and new resolutions. The future lies before us like a field of fresh snow—no tracks or anything to mar its beauty. Forgetting those things which are behind, I press forward toward the mark for the prize of the high calling of God.

I'm trying to forget one thing that's behind me—my summer with Nate—but it's uphill work! Last night I dreamed I was with him in his boat, it was warm, and a huge moon was rising. He held out his hand and begged me to marry him. I desperately wanted to say yes, but just at that moment a terrible storm came along, lightning flashed, thunder crashed, and a mighty wind came up and nearly upset the boat. I awoke with pounding heart and tears in my eyes.

Oh God, give me the heart to put my all into the work here. Strengthen me for my tasks, and give me wisdom. I feel so weak and unfit for this job.

Allen has had some miserable nights. On Friday evening at ten, a noise at the window awakened me out of a sound sleep. I sat up, heart pounding in fear, and there it was again—a sound like a bit of gravel being thrown against the window.

I tiptoed over and peered out the window, and there in the moonlight stood Allen, motioning for me to come down. I opened the window, and he called softly, "Could you come down to the kitchen?"

I quickly dressed with trembling hands that could hardly do the job. Allen was pacing back and forth in the kitchen, an agonizing look on his face.

"Do something for me," he pleaded. "Could you sing for me or pray out loud?"

I thought crying would go better than singing, and also I wasn't sure I could do either. So I got the Bible and read to him from the Psalms. I tried to use a calm, soothing tone, but I could hardly keep my voice from trembling. The Scriptures seemed to calm him, though, and presently he thanked me and went off to bed.

However, sleep was out of the question for me after that. Praying helped, but it still seemed like such a heavy burden on my shoulders. It's up to me to see that he gets medication and help.

So many perplexing problems here. I look back with longing to the time I was at Isaac's. I miss little Matthew so much that it's almost like a tangible hurt in my heart. But overshadowing that are my feelings for Nate and the pain of memories of being with him. Dear Lord, help me!

Eli has left to work a year for one pair of his many uncles and aunts. Since he is fifteen and through going to three-hour school every Saturday, Allen has decided to hire him out. I must admit that in the nearly six weeks I've been here, I haven't learned to know him well. He's quiet and never much in the house. I never got much more out of him than a shy smile.

Clyde and Noah are more outgoing and talkative. On Sunday evening as they were getting ready to go to the singing, I heard Noah teasing Clyde about a certain girl. I hadn't thought of him as old enough yet, even though he's twenty. His build is small and slight, and I can hardly accept that he's only a few years younger than Isaac. I am so glad for the two oldest boys here at home, because Allen often can't work. Having the boys here to do the work relieves him of some stress and strain. ❧

January 8

*T*he hard shell that surrounds Rachel seems to be cracking a little. On Monday evening I was busy in the kitchen, and all the rest of the family was in the living room, playing games and eating popcorn and apples. It was a cozy family scene, and my heart warmed at the sight of it. Maybe my job here wouldn't be so difficult after all. Things were bound to get better, too.

Presently Allen told the little ones to run up to bed, and Mary came to me for her nightgown and her good-night kiss. Dave and Abram called good-night and scrambled up the steps. Then Rachel walked through the kitchen, too, to go upstairs, and I called, "Good-night, Rachel."

Her only answer was to retort in a low voice, "You're trying to hook Dad, and you know it." She turned and fled upstairs without giving me a chance to reply.

My first impulse was to run after her and set her straight right away, but something held me back. I was too angry to talk rationally just then. The strength suddenly went out of my legs, and I sat down weakly in a chair. At least I had all night then to ponder and pray about it before I had to face her again.

Tuesday morning brought the usual rush of getting the

scholars off to school: doing chores, packing lunches, eating breakfast. All day I prayed for Rachel, off and on, and for wisdom for myself to know what to say to her.

When she came home from school, she went straight up to her room. I gave Mary the job of folding handkerchiefs, and the boys ran out to the barn. Then I went upstairs and knocked on Rachel's door.

A muffled voice answered, "What do you want?"

"May I come in?" I asked.

No answer.

I opened the door slightly. "I need to talk to you."

"What did I do wrong now?" she asked.

I went into her room and closed the door. She was sprawled on her bed, and I sat down on the edge of it.

"Rachel," I pleaded. "Why can't we be friends?"

She covered her face with her hands and began to cry. "I want my mother," she sobbed.

My thoughts and feelings churned. What could I say?

"I know you want your mother," I finally comforted her, stroking her hair gently, "and someday you can be with her again if you live the way she would want you to live. Don't you think she'd want you to be cheerful and obedient? Perhaps she can see you and is wishing you'd be able to brace up and accept things as they are.

"And Rachel, I'm not trying to 'hook' your dad. Did you notice that he's not feeling very well? I feel sorry for him and wish we could do something to help him. It would really help him a lot if you'd be cheerful and friendly."

She didn't respond at all, but the rest of the day she seemed more relaxed and submissive. I spent the evening telling the children Bible stories. They listened, wide eyed, and when I stopped, they begged for more. 🌿

*T*onight I went for a walk in the cold snow. Dave and Abram came running out of the barn, and I asked them if they'd like to go along, too. I pointed out the big dipper to them, and we stood gazing into the clear, star-studded sky.

"Is Mama up there in heaven?" Abram asked wistfully.

I squeezed his hand. "She's with Jesus. Would you like to show me the animals you have in your barn?"

We toured the barn, then, and Dave proudly showed me his bunnies and all the other animals. The barn is a warm, friendly place, and it's no wonder the boys like to play there.

As we were walking back to the house, Abram squeezed my hand and said, "I like you."

That put warm circles around my heart. ❦

*T*his afternoon I drove to Dr. Wing's office. He is such a good-natured, kindhearted, wise old doctor. In a short time I was unburdening to him, telling him about Allen, and asking him for advice about Grandma and Allen. He gave me a packet of pills for Allen, which should help tide him over this rough time of learning to adjust to life without Frieda.

Frieda was the sunshine and song in this home, shedding joy for all, and he loved her more than life itself. The children miss her sorely. How poor a substitute I am for their own dear mother!

Oh, Lord help me to be a channel of your love in this home. Help me to gladly and cheerfully serve them, and therein find healing for the pain in my own heart.

As for Grandma, since she is needed so much yet, we decided it would be best to have her stay, and pray for a miracle of more time for her, if it is God's will. Our heavenly Father is all-wise and all-knowing, and he causes everything to work together for good to those who love him and serve him. 🌿

February 18

*A*llen is much better, and now I know what he looks like when he smiles or chuckles. He seems like a different man.

Yesterday two of his brothers and their wives were here helping to butcher a hog. That was something new for me, because years ago it never took much meat for just my parents and me. It was really interesting—scalding the hog, scraping the hide, cutting and taking care of the meat, and cooking the lard. They kept a jolly, interesting conversation going. I really enjoyed the day together, and now I'm looking forward to the butchering of the beef.

On Sunday afternoon I was upstairs in my room, reading, when I heard the sound of carriage wheels on the gravel in the lane below. I looked out the window and was overjoyed to see Isaac, Rosemary, and Matthew driving in. I flew down the steps and ran out to usher them into the house.

Matthew ran to me and cried, "Mammy! Mammy!"

I picked him up and hugged him and we both laughed

and cried together. Isaac was a sight for sore eyes, too—so joyously dear and good-looking. Rosemary positively glowed with inner happiness and outward beauty and graciousness.

What a delightful afternoon we had, talking and reminiscing! Allen was in a talkative mood, and Grandma outdid herself with kindness and friendliness. It truly was an afternoon that satisfied my longing for companionship and fellowship with dear and good friends.

When they prepared to leave, I had to quench an almost irresistible longing to get my shawl and bonnet, and go along, too. How foolish is my heart! 🌿

March 9

I decided that, before I start housecleaning, I'll be able to quilt the four-patch quilt which Rachel pieced together over the winter months. So last week I pinned it into the frame. It's really pretty, and I told Rachel so. She beamed with quiet happiness.

Something happened a few weeks ago that helped change Rachel. I was sewing in the living room and suddenly remembered that it was high time to put wood on the fire. I called out, "Rachel, would you mind putting a chunk of wood on the fire?"

Her quick reply was "No, you can do it yourself!"

Unknown to her, Grandma had just come out of the bedroom and overheard. "Rachel," she said, "come over here and sit beside me for a few minutes."

I heard the stove lid being opened and closed, and Rachel walking over to Grandma. While I continued sewing, I couldn't help but overhear their conversation. Before Grandma could say more, Rachel burst out, "Oh Grandma, I try so hard to be good, but I just can't be! I pray for help, but God doesn't hear my prayers."

She began to cry, great heart-wrenching sobs that made me pity her with my whole heart. I could hardly see to sew anymore because of my own tears, and I prayed for Grandma to be able to say something that would help Rachel.

Grandma let her cry for a few minutes, and then she said, "Rachel, I want you to know that God loves you very much. He loves you more than your mother loved you. He knows how hard you are trying, and he sees your every tear.

"The Bible tells us that God will not despise a broken spirit and a contrite heart. He also knows how much you miss your mother, and how hard it is to do without her. God wants to be your best friend, Rachel, if you will let him.

"Every time you do or say something you shouldn't, stop right away and ask the Lord to forgive you. Tell him you're sorry you've grieved him, and ask for his strength to do better. The Lord will help you to overcome sin and live in obedience. It's also good to go to the person you've wronged and tell her you're sorry and ask for forgiveness."

The boys came in just then, and the conversation was ended. But that evening as I was preparing for bed, there was a tap on my door, and Rachel edged into the room. She timidly said, "I'm sorry I talked back to you."

I drew her close and assured her that it was all right. We had a little heart-to-heart talk, and since then we've felt especially close. Daily I praise and thank God for this. Now Rachel is so easy to love and eager to please.

Every afternoon these days I've been spending time at the quilt until the scholars come home from school, and Grandma sits close by. She is such a consecrated Christian and has deep insights into spiritual matters. I've been an eager pupil, asking questions and learning much from her.

On Friday Noah came in for a drink while we were in the midst of a discussion about spiritual matters, and he joined in the conversation. He is thinking of taking the instruction class for baptism and joining church, and he asked some questions, too. I think that having to lose their mother has made the children more serious-minded than most young people.

"One thing I can't understand," he mused. "Salvation is said to be a free gift, and yet good works such as obedience, self-denial, and abiding by church rules are required." Noah was sitting backward astride a chair, his hat far back on his head, and a sincere, puzzled look on his face. I could see that he was not merely trying to be flippant or sarcastic, and I was so glad Grandma was there to try to explain.

She started out: "The Bible says that all have sinned and come short of the glory of God. The wages of sin is eternal death. There is no way we could be good enough to earn our own salvation.

"Christ died on the cross and paid the price for our sin, bringing us salvation and hope. We need to meet the conditions for receiving this gift."

Grandma paused and closed her eyes, as if in rest.

"What are the conditions for receiving it?" Noah asked. I think he knew but wanted to hear Grandma say it again.

She quietly stated, "The Scriptures call us to believe in Christ and receive him as the ruler of our lives. He is our

Redeemer and shows the way for us to follow. We must repent of all known sin and forsake it, surrendering our all to Christ in obedience to his commands and submission to the church.

"We can come to Christ because our heavenly Father draws us to him. No matter how much someone has sinned, Christ will not turn away anyone who sincerely comes to him, meets these requirements, and asks for forgiveness and salvation."

Clyde had come in looking for Noah. Not wanting to interrupt Grandma's speech, he sat quietly on the settee, listening, too. When she paused, Clyde asked, "Can we be sure we are saved, or would that lead to pride?"

Grandma replied, "We must never doubt God's Word. If we confess our sins, God is faithful and just to forgive us our sins. The one who confesses and forsakes sin, finds mercy. God is faithful and just in keeping his Word, and he protects us from Satan.

"But if we depart from Christ and choose a life of sin, we are no longer under God's grace. We can expect new mercy only by responding to the Spirit in true repentance and returning to Christ.

"Salvation is our blessed hope if we endure to the end. As long as we live, we need to continue in humility, obedience, and yieldedness to Christ and our brothers and sisters in the church."

I could see that Grandma was tiring, but the boys seemed sincerely interested. I hadn't the heart to suggest that they let Grandma rest now.

"What does it mean to be born again?" Clyde asked

With effort Grandma spoke again: "When we surrender self and come to Christ, accepting him as our Savior, then we are born into God's family. He makes us one of his children, and he is our heavenly Father. He gives us a new nature that no longer delights in sin, but strives for holiness, and we are new creatures in Christ.

"We were born as babies into our natural family, and as we grow up, we learn to fit in. When we become Christians, we are born into our spiritual family by the work of the Holy Spirit and by the water of the washing of regeneration. Then we learn to live in accord with that church family. I believe this is what is meant by the new birth."

The scholars burst into the kitchen just then, filling the room with their lively chatter, and the older boys went back to work. I escaped to my room to quickly write down all that she said so I wouldn't forget it. Now I've recopied it into my diary. I feel it's a priceless opportunity to be taught by one of God's dear saints.

The wind is howling around the corners of the house tonight. "O Wind, if winter comes, can spring be far behind?" (P. B. Shelley).

April 15

*A*h spring! Green grass, warm balmy breezes, sunshine, and flowers. Lo, the winter, with all its frustrations and tears, is over and gone, and the time of the singing of birds is come. How full is my heart tonight!

This morning as I stood at the kitchen sink washing dishes, I spied a familiar-looking team coming in the lane. Could it be possible? Was it really Polly Mast?

It was, indeed, and what an enjoyable day we had, chatting and working together. We finished the housecleaning and did some baking.

Polly is so jolly and comfortable that the children warmed to her in no time. Even Allen, who is usually somewhat reserved, visited freely with her at the dinner table. I will cherish this day in my memory as long as I live.

Grandma and Mary took naps this afternoon, so we were working alone. I couldn't resist asking about Nate. . . . "How is your cousin Nate doing?"

"I've no report of Nate and Hannah going with each other, if that's what you want to know!"

I looked out the window so Polly wouldn't see my face. Why do I feel so glad? Shame on me!

"In fact," Polly said, "the neighbors haven't seen much of Nate all winter."

Hmmmm. . . . I wonder if he's well. If it would be proper, I'd write to him. But that would never do.

Another bit of news from Polly gave me a jolt: a few days ago, Priscilla gave birth to a baby daughter. I have sober thoughts. Alone, poor child! I must remember to pray for her and the baby. I'm so glad she has an uncle and aunt who took her in. I want to write her a letter, and I'll still do it today, if possible.

Oh God, give me the wisdom to know what to write that would be a help to her. 🌿

May 10

*B*lossom time! One of my favorite times of the year! Mary and I spent the day working outside, mowing, trimming, and weeding the garden.

Mary is my shadow, a real question box. I'm becoming hopelessly attached to her, and I'm afraid it will be as hard to leave her as it was for me to leave Matthew. What fun to comb her golden hair, to watch her blue eyes light up when something delights her! She has features of exquisite delicacy and refinement, and her feelings flit across her face in total transparency.

The other day she happened to step on a beautiful butterfly in the garden. Perhaps it was grounded because it had already been injured, but Mary couldn't get over the fact that she had killed it. There was a tragic expression on her face, and two big tears slid down her cheeks.

To cheer her, I told her that maybe she and I and Grandma could have a picnic all by ourselves under the blossoming pear tree. She sure brightened up then and ran to pack sandwiches, cookies, and fruit. Allen was away for the day. We pushed Grandma in her wheelchair out under the tree, and it really was a lovely picnic.

The lilac bush in the yard is blooming, filling the air with delightful scents. On the north side of the house, fragrant little lilies of the valley are modestly giving forth their sweetness, bees drone busily among the flowers, and the garden is a real picture. Such peace and serenity!

I thought about Frieda. Is she perhaps now in a heavenly garden, among winding streams and beautiful flowers and shrubbery (with no bugs nor thorns and thistles!), singing praises to her Savior?

We will never know until we reach that shining shore, for the Bible says that eyes have not seen and ears have not heard what is prepared for those who love God. 🌿

*P*eas and strawberry time! What good eating we have these days! Fresh lettuce and radishes from the garden, too. Dave and Abram each have a little plot of ground for their very own garden. They take an interest in gardening, and it's surprising how much they know about when it's time to set out tomato, melon, and cucumber plants. . . .

Today they spent several hours working in their gardens. Then with shining eyes and big smiles, they came in to ask me out to see them. Abram pulled at my hand, so eager was he to show me his pride and joy.

It was something to see! Perfectly weedfree, neat rows of healthy looking plants! Dave's plot was bordered with marigolds, and Abram's with periwinkle. I could hardly believe how nice it all looked, and I praised them lavishly.

It's a good thing, I believe, that they have such an interest in gardening. For one thing, gardening keeps them out of mischief for a while, and with it we can cultivate their interest in farming later on.

I'm glad the children now accept me so completely and trust and appreciate me. Grandma is holding her own, and Allen is his usual self. Time heals all wounds, they say. I would change that to: God heals all wounds if we let him.

It's good to be busy, as we have been. The men are getting ready for haying in a few weeks. In the house, we're canning quart after quart of peas, strawberries, and rhubarb. It gives us a feeling of satisfaction and accomplishment to see the work disappear, and having the health and strength to be able to do it.

Thank you, Lord, for your bountiful blessings.

 What is so rare as a day in June?" (J. R. Lowell). Lovely, sweet, fragrant roses. Honey-suckle-laden road banks. Blue skies. What beautiful gifts God gives us on our often-weary and tiresome journey heavenward!

Grandma has left us, and how we all miss her. She decided to go and live with her daughter, perhaps for her remaining days. She says she is homesick for heaven, her soul longs for it, and she feels that her wish will be granted before too long.

All spring Allen has been helping me with the milking, both morning and evening. I feel that it was a battle won for him, quite a victory, and a sign of healing, a healthy step in the grief process. When I first came, he thought he could not bear it, because when Frieda was here, milking was their special time to talk. But now he helps milk and even confides freely in me, and we often have heart-to-heart talks.

Allen is thoughtful and considerate of me, and he goes out of his way to do small favors for me. As I ponder his kind deeds, I'm afraid he's beginning to have "feelings" for me, feelings that perhaps I won't be able to return. Must he go through another heartache? Or is it God's will? Perhaps it's just the foolish imaginings of my heart. . . .

At any rate, I'll put the thought out of my head, live one day at a time, and wait for God's guidance. 🌿

*B*irthdays are
like stepping-stones
Along life's winding hills:
Special little vantage points
To pause and just stand still;
To look back over other times,
Recall the bygone years;
Reliving all the memories,
The smiles, the joys, the tears;
Then, to leave past backward views
And start to climb once more,
With faith that years ahead will be
As full as those before. (Unknown)

Am I really forty-two years old already? Time is flying like a weaver's shuttle. Life is such a transient thing. We try to grasp life and find that it is but a vapor. Oh, may we all live so that, should we be taken from this life in the twinkling of an eye, we would be prepared to joyfully meet God!

Today I thoroughly cleaned the entire kitchen. I scrubbed, polished, and waxed until everything shone. Then I got out my rolling pin and flour, sugar, and some more of Grandma's no-no's, and made five delicious raspberry pies. Since Grandma is gone, the family is regularly demanding pies, cookies, and desserts.

Now I'm sitting here on the rocker, writing in my diary, and feeling a little lonely. I must admit that I was eagerly watching for the mail carrier, anticipating a birthday card or a letter. But the mail came, and there was nothing for me.

Not a single soul thought of me! Oh well, I'm not a child anymore. I guess this afternoon I'll go and visit a neighbor lady, Mrs. Frey. She's a sweet, kind old lady, nearly ninety, and as far as I know, never receives any mail or gets any company. She is a Christian, although not Amish.

• • •

Evening: I did go and visit Mrs. Frey, and I believe it was of the Spirit's leading. Several times I knocked loudly on the door since she's hard of hearing, but there was no answer. Then from inside I heard a faint cry for help. I quickly went in, and there she was, lying on the floor and unable to get up, poor soul.

She told me to call her son (luckily she knew the telephone number), and I also called for an ambulance. Her son and his wife were there in a few minutes. They kept saying over and over how sorry they were that they hadn't called at lunchtime.

I decided I was no longer needed at that pathetic scene, so I left. I called on several more neighbors, and when I came home an hour later, I found another pitiful scene. Rachel was lying on the sofa, face down, crying heartbrokenly. (Why does she take the difficulties of life, both big and small, with such intense feeling?)

"I wanted to bake you a birthday cake," she sobbed, "and it flopped."

Only then did I notice a rather flat-looking cake on the counter.

"And that Clyde!" she cried reproachfully. "He came in and saw it and asked if I sat on it." More tears and sniffles.

With admirable self-control, I didn't laugh, but told her that she could try again, and I would help her. And so we had a lovely frosted birthday cake for supper, and a happy girl once again. The pigs enjoyed the flopped cake, judging by the speed with which they devoured it.

After the children were in bed, Allen was reading the farm paper while I tidied up the kitchen. I was about to head up the stairs when Allen called out, "Wait a minute! I want to give you something." He went into the sitting room and came out with a large, wrapped package.

"It's your birthday present," he said, smiling shyly. "You've done so much for us all, and I can't find the words to tell you how much I appreciate it."

With eager, trembling fingers I undid the wrapping. Inside was a lovely ceramic bowl-and-pitcher set, creamy white, with blue flowers on it.

"Oh!" I exclaimed, "it's really beautiful! Something I've always wanted. Thank you!"

I think he was pleased at my pleasure with the gift, and we sat at the table and talked for about an hour before going to bed.

I'm so glad that his wounds have healed and that he has recovered so well. When I think back to Christmastime, I realize what a miracle has happened, an answer to prayer!

Now I feel like part of the family, and each member of the family is becoming increasingly dear to me. How could I bear it to be parted from them? ✀

July 1

*B*eautiful, summer days, filled with work, play, and laughter, and sometimes tears, passing in swift succession. Grandma was here for a visit yesterday. I wanted to throw my arms around her and implore her to stay, but I know it's best this way.

The children were glad to see her, too. Mary wanted to climb all over her, which is too tiring for Grandma, so I told her to go, pick a bouquet of pretty flowers for her. She came in with her arms full of them, and I arranged them in my birthday pitcher, which I have sitting on the kitchen sideboard temporarily, for all to see. The flowers are extra pretty this year—a gift of God to cheer us on our earthly pilgrimage.

On Sunday our district had no church and we had an invitation to Isaac and Rosemary's for the afternoon. The service was to be at a farm next to theirs. How I enjoyed the day, seeing dear, familiar friends in church, and sitting beside Mamie Lapp once more! It was good to hear Preacher Dan and Amos expound the Scriptures again. Dan chose John 15 for his text, and he spoke much about yielding our lives to God and bringing forth fruit. How I long to be a fruitful vine in his vineyard, to be continually abiding in Christ! There are so many distractions, and so often I fall short.

After the service, we visited during the light lunch and later slipped away, following Isaac and Rosemary to their place. Seeing my former home agai   brought back many precious memories, my dear kitchen where I used to prepare the meals, and the yard and garden I took care of. Again Matthew ran joyously to his "Mammy," and stayed close by me all afternoon. Isaac and Rosemary were gracious and friendly, and they served us a watermelon on the lawn. Before I was ready, it was time to go home.

Since we drive right past Polly Mast's place, we stopped in there, too, and oh my, what a reception we got! She insisted that we stay for supper, which we could do since the older boys were at home handling the chores. We ate out under her trees, by the stream, and talked and visited like old times. The children waded in the brook, and Allen enjoyed our company, even though he was the only man there.

What a sweet, friendly day! It's so easy to be happy when we're with dear, good friends that enrich and hallow our lives. We drove home in the starry, summer-scented twilight, feeling at peace with the world and its folks. ✿

July 2

I can still hardly believe it's true, but I have to. There, along the kitchen wall beside the sideboard, stands a little white crib, which Noah carried down from the attic, and in it lies a sleeping baby!

After lunch, while I was at the kitchen sink washing dishes, a car drove in, and a young woman carrying a baby walked toward the house. The figure looked familiar, but not until she came closer did I recognize Priscilla. She walked in without knocking and swiftly came over and handed the baby to me!

"Here, take little Dora," she whispered hoarsely. "I can't care for her anymore."

"What?" I asked blankly.

"I mean it," she insisted. "Will you raise her for me?"

"I—I don't know. Maybe I could care her for a while."

"No," she said. "For always. I know you'll be good to her. I—I'm sick. . . . I'm dying."

I stared at Priscilla. Suddenly I noticed how tired and

haggard she looked, and there were dark circles under her eyes. Was it really true? I don't know, for as quickly as she had come in, she walked out. Her driver came to the door with a big box of baby clothes and diapers and formula and bottles, and he too turned right around and headed for the car.

Quickly I came to my senses. I laid the baby on the sofa, called Mary to watch her, and hurried out after Priscilla.

"Wait," I called. "Let's talk some more. Where will you be? Where are you going?"

"I'm on my way to the hospital," she said, showing no emotion. "I know you'll take good care of my baby and raise her to be a fine Christian girl. We have to go now."

They drove off in a cloud of dust, and I stood there speechless, staring after them. Then I slowly walked to the house. Little Dora was crying, and Mary was juggling her up and down to quiet her. I still wasn't able to comprehend it all. Allen and the boys came in from the barn wondering what the commotion was all about.

"What shall I do?" I asked Allen, after I had told him the whole story. "Shall we keep her?"

"I suppose so, for the time being," he answered. "Before long we'll have to talk with her mother and the aunt and uncle, and see what they think."

"Look!" cried Rachel, who had been rummaging through the baby's supplies. She held up a paper.

"It's a birth certificate," Allen said, taking it from her. I looked it over, too. The date of her birth was April tenth, which makes her nearly three months old. Allen put the birth certificate inside the big family Bible in the sitting room.

Finally I had a chance to really look at "my" baby. Dark,

curly hair, big wandering eyes, in a small, heart-shaped face. Tiny, grasping fists. Suddenly I was overwhelmed with emotion, only I didn't know whether to laugh or cry. Not every day is one left holding a baby! I'm beginning to let myself be happy and excited about it. What a solemn responsibility! In God's sight, her life is priceless for all eternity, and our task is to teach, to train, to mold her.

Oh, I wish I knew what God's will is for us all! Will I stay and marry Allen? I suspect that's what he has in mind. Is that God's will? Yet my heart is still aching for Nate. Is God preparing me to forget Nate? Perhaps at this very moment, he and Hannah are making their wedding plans.

Whatever God's will is for me, that's what I want, whether it's to stay single, or marry Allen, or Nate, or someone else. As long as I'm in the center of God's will, that is happiness for me. I need not fret nor worry. In due time God will make known his will. He will guide me. That is the blessed privilege of being his child, a daughter of the King. What can I want beside? 🌸

July 30

*H*aving a baby in the house makes a lot more work, but it's wonderful! Rachel and Mary vie for the chance to hold her and give her the bottle, or wheel her around outside in the baby carriage. Even the big boys can't walk past her without trying some baby talk on her and patting her cheek.

Allen and I went to the hospital to visit Priscilla on Friday evening. I hoped I'd get a chance to talk with one of her doctors, but I didn't. Is it true that she's going to die soon?

She seemed glad for visitors and told us to come again and bring Dora along. Allen talked to her about the condition of her soul and stressed the importance of everyone, even those in the best of health, being prepared to die.

She answered, "I'm ready to meet God. I've given my life to him and repented. I've been wayward, and it took this illness to bring me back. I wish I could be healed." She closed her eyes and a tear slipped down her cheek.

"Perhaps God will heal you," I said, squeezing her hand. She didn't open her eyes again, and we tiptoed softly out the door. ✄

August 10

*B*aby's four months old today. She coos and gurgles and baby-talks, charming us all. Yesterday Priscilla's mother came to see the baby. She's really nice after one gets to know and understand her. I asked about Priscilla's condition. She said it's some kind of a blood disorder—nothing contagious—and the doctors say it could go either way: she could get better, or it could get worse and be fatal.

She also said Priscilla has made application for coming back to the church, and they'll be having council about it on the next church Sunday. I'm so glad to hear of this move. ✄

*T*oday it's one year ago that Frieda died. Allen has been rather quiet all day. I believe it's a day filled with sad memories for him. Also, that kicker cow that I dreaded milking so much when I first came here—it gave him an unexpected whack this morning and sent him flying. Now he has sore ribs, and he spent most of the day on the sofa. He declared that the cow will be sent to the livestock auction first thing Monday morning!

It's been a busy summer: all the work (or rather play) involved in taking care of little Dora, plus the canning and freezing of our bounteous garden yields, and the usual cooking, baking, cleaning, laundering, yard, garden, and barn chores. The children helped well, and everyone seemed happy and well adjusted. It's an answer to prayer.

I'm holding Dora as I write. She seems to be prettier every day. I believe it's good for Mary to have another little cutie in the house and have to share the limelight. Perhaps it will keep her from becoming too spoiled and from getting all the attention. Seeing them together makes people talk of the contrast: Mary so blonde, blue-eyed, and round-cheeked; and Dora's dark blue, almost violet, eyes, dark curls, and heart-shaped face.

I have to keep reminding myself that it's what's inside that counts. There's an almost painful feeling in my heart when I wonder if Dora has inherited the nature of her grandfather or her parents.

Oh God, as long as Dora is in my care, help me to teach and live and train and discipline her well, and according to your will, so that when she's old she will not depart from the right way. ❦

*F*irst week of school! This year Abram's going, too, and he's having a hard time adjusting to it. On Monday morning he seemed eager enough to go. He looked so cute with his new yellow shirt and home-made pants, his face scrubbed clean and hair neatly combed, carrying his new lunch bucket, which I had filled with good things to eat.

He's so full of life and mischief at home that I wondered whether he'd be able to keep it under control at school. Imagine my surprise when at first recess he came home sniffling, and then said he's never going back. A short time later, Dave came running home, breathless and panting, looking for Abram. They couldn't find him at school, so Teacher sent Dave to find him.

With much sweet talk and cajoling, we finally got him persuaded to go along with Dave again. It went fairly well the rest of the day, according to Rachel. But the next morning he refused to get ready for school. Allen wasn't at home, and I wished for more experience to know how to handle Abram. Then I thought of prayer. I knelt right beside his bed where he lay, hiding his face in the covers. When I looked up, he was staring curiously at me.

"Why are you saying your prayers now?" he asked.

"Because I want *den guten Herr* to help me," I replied, "to show you that you should be a big brave boy and go to school and learn."

"Does the good Lord want me to go to school?" he asked dubiously.

"Yes, indeed he does. And he will help you to be brave and strong."

"Then I will!" he said courageously, and promptly began getting ready. There were a few more episodes like that later in the week, but he won the victory over those, too.

Thank you, Lord. 🥀

*T*here is autumn in the air. I wish I'd be a real writer so I could find the words to express it. That sweet, half-sad tang in the air. Misty early mornings and mellow sunshine. That autumny fragrance, and leaves changing color. The bright splash of color of the yellow and gold marigolds. A hummingbird darting in and out of the red firebranch flowers.

I put Dora in her stroller, propped her up with pillows, and took her and Mary for a walk. We were so busy canning pears yesterday that I felt we deserved a little break. It did us good to see the outdoors of nature, God's handiwork. We stopped for a few minutes to chat with Mrs. Frey, who is now in a wheelchair and has someone with her all the time. She's a dear soul, and I came away feeling refreshed and counting my blessings.

Tonight I got all the children to write letters to Eli once again. I have no way of knowing what temptations he may be facing, so far away from home, or whether he was ever homesick or longing for his mother. I keep reminding the children to pray for him every evening in their bedtime prayers.

The sweetest time of day for me is when the younger ones gather around me and kneel to say their prayers, after we read a Bible story together. Their prayers are so original, fresh, and innocent. Dave: "Dear God, help my rabbit to get lots of little bunnies and don't let them die." Mary: "Thank you for letting us have Dora and Miriam." Last night Abram surprised me with his prayer: "Please make Dad ask Miriam to stay here always." Then he looked up and smiled a most mischievous smile at me. His two front teeth are missing, and it gives him a naughty look.

If I would have to leave them, how would I ever be able to be happy again? I'm glad to put everything in God's hands. At first I didn't want to come here, but now I'm glad I did, and I don't like to think of leaving. I'm so glad that God knows what's best for us all.

Even though I needed to give up my own will, this should yield the peaceable fruit of righteousness. The peace of knowing I am at the center of God's will, which passes all understanding, is worth more than any earthly gain or prestige, or even a multitude of friends. I hear Jesus saying, My peace I give unto you, my child.

October 8

We just received the happy news today that Isaac and Rosemary have a baby daughter named Rosabeth. I think that's nice—she's partly named after her mother and partly after Matthew's mother, Elizabeth. I can hardly wait to see the wee girlie. She's almost exactly a half year younger than Dora. Will they be good friends someday?

Dora is growing and developing nicely, starting to crawl, and I'm afraid she won't be a baby much longer. The very thought of parting with her frightens me, and I hope God won't ask me to do that. But, if he does, he'll help me give her up, I know. Yet the mother heart in me cries out, Perish the thought!

On Sunday evening we had some special company for supper. Sylvia, Clyde's girlfriend, was here. She is two years older than he, and friendly, capable, and outgoing. They have been dating for eight months now, and I wouldn't be surprised to hear talk of wedding before long. Clyde was twenty-one in April, and her dad wants to retire and let them take over the farm.

All evening I was thinking of Sylvia in terms of "my future daughter-in-law." When I realized what I was doing, I gave myself a sound scolding. The very nerve of me! ✥

October 16

*T*oday was a memorable yet disturbing day. We packed picnic snacks and drove to church in Isaac's district. It was so pleasant to gather with my friends, so soul-satisfying and dear to my heart. This was the first time I was there with little Dora, and everyone wanted to look at her.

I feel more at home with the congregation there than in Allen's district. Is it because the people are a little plainer or more friendly? Perhaps. Anyhow, I could hardly tear away from visiting after the light lunch. When I got to the carriage, everyone was packed in already, and waiting. We wanted to have an outing along the creek.

"Just where are we going?" Mary asked, bouncing up and down eagerly.

"Wait and see," Allen replied, winking at me. Dear familiar country roads. My heart skipped a beat when we drove into Nate's long lane. Allen was grinning from ear to ear.

I wish I'd know what he'd heard about Nate and me, and why he took me there. I had not seen Nate at church, and apparently he wasn't at home either. Perhaps he drove to another district. I wonder if Allen intended for Nate to see us together, picnicking there, and surmise from it that we belong to each other. I can't figure it out.

We walked along the creek for about a half mile until we found a shady, secluded spot. It was so beautiful there, golden leaves falling into the water from the tall trees overhead, and it brought back many precious memories. I decided I wouldn't let myself feel sad. Why should I feel sad if God is directing my life? But being there along Nate's beloved creek had an emotional effect on me.

We ate our carrot and celery sticks, apples, and cookies. Then the children ran off to explore the creek banks and wade in the shallow water that, surprisingly, was still warm enough. To feed Dora, I sat on a spread-out carriage blanket with my back against a tree. Allen walked off, too, and Dora soon fell asleep in the comfortable nest I made for her on the blanket.

I stretched out beside Dora. It was so peaceful and serene that in no time I was sleeping, too, and dreaming. I dreamed Nate came out of his house and stood in his yard, shading his eyes from the sun with his hand, and was looking over at me. I motioned for him to come over, and he started walking toward me. Closer and closer came his footsteps, and then he stood beside me, looking down at me.

My eyes flew open, and there stood Allen smiling down

at me. I sat up quickly, and he sat down cross-legged on the edge of the blanket, carefully so as not to awaken Dora. He cleared his throat, and said, "I think it's about time we make some plans for the future."

Oh no, not now! I thought wildly. The dream was still vivid in my mind. My heart still wasn't beating normally. Dora stirred, and my thoughts turned to her. Would her mother want her back? Did Allen think I was using his money to pay for her formula? Now was the time to talk about it.

"I wanted to talk to you about Dora for a while already," I told him. "I haven't used your money for any of her needs. I'm paying her expenses with my own money. You have enough with your own family."

"I can't see that it makes much difference," he said impatiently, waving his hand. "As long as she needs a home, I won't turn her out."

"Priscilla is better," I continued, "and out of the hospital. I'm afraid one day she'll come and take her back."

"Oh" was all he said. It was plain to see he wasn't much interested in talking about Dora and Priscilla.

"It's us I want to talk about," he suddenly blurted out.

"On my part," I responded hastily, "there's nothing to say. I'm waiting on God's leading in my life. Whatever his will is, that's what I want. I'll do nothing different until he makes his will known."

What possessed me to say that, when I sensed in my heart he was about to propose? Why was I so hasty and self-righteous? I've been reproaching myself ever since!

"I'm not surprised you aren't married yet," Allen commented as he got up and walked off.

There's a great sense of loss in my heart, almost as if I

had trampled underfoot something fine and good. I've been undecided since. Should I go to him and say, I'm sorry I said what I did, and I want to hear what you were going to say? Why is my heart holding me back? Oh God, forgive me, and help me to know what I should do. I've felt unhappy and irritable ever since. Where is your perfect peace, that peace which passes all understanding?

We left to visit Isaac's a short time later. Rosabeth is a sweet, adorable baby, beautiful and perfectly formed. Being in the state of mind that I was, I almost felt resentful of Isaac and Rosemary's happiness. But on the way home, I was ashamed of myself, and I was as contrite as could be. After all that Isaac went through! What's wrong with me, anyway? Why do I feel so restless and heart-hungry?

Oh God, help me to feel your presence and to be at peace with the world and myself again. ✻

November 3

*D*ear, familiar diary! For weeks I thought I'd never write another word in you. Trying to write while flat on my back isn't the easiest thing, but the nurse helped me to prop it up on a pillow. I can't remember much of the accident, but parts of it are coming back.

On October 17, Allen hitched up to take me to the grocery store. I am so thankful now that I left Dora and Mary at home. If Noah hadn't come in just then and offered to babysit, we would've taken them along. We hadn't gone more than a mile when a car hit the buggy—on my side. The driver had fallen asleep. Allen wasn't hurt, but I woke up in the hospital.

I had a slight concussion and a badly broken leg. I don't remember much of that first week—just one pain-filled day after another. On one of my worst days, Nate Mast came to visit me. He seemed ill at ease in the hospital surroundings. Perhaps he had never seen a woman in bed with her leg in traction. I was too hazy even to hold a conversation. I'm sure it was a big relief to him to leave.

Polly Mast is taking my place at Allen's until I'm able to work again. Allen and the children take turns visiting me, and Polly came several times, too. Last time Rachel was here I told her to send my diary along next time someone comes. Clyde brought it last night.

He had big news to tell me. He and Sylvia are getting married on the first Thursday of December! He apologized for not telling me sooner, but they just planned it a few weeks ago themselves. I told him I'm happy for them and wished him the Lord's blessing on their marriage.

It seems like all my restless and impatient feelings I had before the accident are gone. Perhaps this being laid up was a chastening of the Lord, to humble me, his voice telling me, "Be still and know that I am God."

Why did I stew and fret, instead of trusting the Lord? He can take even our errors and blunders, and redeem them, and still turn things around for his honor and glory, and our good. Truly, God does all things well. ✿

November 11

*P*riscilla came to visit me this afternoon. She is excited about her plans. She has been over to talk with Polly, and she says Polly is enthused about the idea, too. She wants the two of us to live in Polly's house together with Dora until my leg is healed and I'm able to walk again. Then I'll work for Allen again, and Polly will move back. Priscilla says I can take Dora with me back to Allen's again, then, for she's afraid her life won't be long anymore. She feels certain that Allen and I will marry, and she wants us to have Dora.

"Time will tell," I told Priscilla mildly. But I gave my consent to her plans about living in Polly's house if she will work out the necessary arrangements. She is looking a lot better, but who knows how long it will last? ✻

November 12

*A*llen was here to visit me this afternoon. He seems to be in good spirits and agreed quite readily to Priscilla's plan for us to live in Polly's house during my recovery.

"Polly was able to step right in and take over without difficulty. The children like her, and everything's going smoothly."

I felt a little stab of something in my heart, that I could be replaced so easily. But all in all, I'm very glad for them.

"I really yearn to see Dave, Abram, Mary, and Dora," I said.

"Then I'll just try to arrange to have them brought in," Allen replied as he said good-bye and wished me well.

I'm getting cards and letters almost every day, which is great pastime for me. In *Die Botschaft*, someone called for a shower of cheer-up messages for me, and now I'm finding out how many friends I really have.

Someone sent me a poem entitled "Shut in with God." That's what I'd like, to make this a time of Bible study and prayer, of continual communion and deeper fellowship with my Savior, to grow spiritually. When I was ill and in pain, all I could do was to whimper to God for help. But now it's different.

The nurses are jolly and friendly—a nicer bunch I couldn't wish for. And Dr. Meighan is courteous and polite. He says that in a few days I may be able to go home.

Home? What is home now? I believe I can understand why Grandma is homesick for heaven. ✍

November 14

*P*olly brought Dave, Abram, and Mary in to visit me tonight. How dear and precious they all looked to me! It was almost more than I could bear not to go along home when they left. Mary jumped upon the bed and hugged me, and the boys stood beside the bed smiling shyly.

Polly said she's glad Priscilla and I will be moving into her house. She'd been worried about someone breaking in and stealing her things, and the house falling into a state of disrepair. Polly insists that she'll charge no rent and even suggested that she should pay us for house-sitting! She urged me to use whatever we need of her supplies.

I am beginning to look forward to getting out of the hospital and going to her place. Hopefully it will be tomorrow! ✍

I'm snuggled comfortably on Polly's sofa, covered with one of her afghans. What an interesting house this is. Bookcases are filled with inspiring Christian books. I've started reading *Light from Heaven*. How fast time flies when I have an interesting book!

Priscilla is putting supper on the table, and Dora is running around in her walker. I came "home" yesterday afternoon. Mrs. Frey's son drove me. We stopped in at Allen's to pick up Dora. She still knew me, and she wiggled all over with delight to see me again.

When we got to Polly's house, Priscilla was already there. Rosemary's sister Ruth had come and cleaned the house and had a fire going, so we had a cheerful welcome. I felt tired and blue, but tried to hide it and be cheerful for Priscilla's sake. Was it because along Nate's road we met Nate and Hannah driving together, laughing and talking to each other, not even noticing me?

Oh dear! I thought I was over that. How can I feel sad so soon after having surrendered my heart, soul, and life to God anew, thinking I have the victory over self? I suppose this dying to self is something that I must do every day. As Paul said, "I die daily." How nice if it could be done once and for all! But it's a lifelong battle, a continual warfare not to let self be on the throne. I keep reminding myself that I am a daughter of the King, and he will not leave me comfortless. 🌿

I don't have much to do besides reading, writing, entertaining Dora, talking with Priscilla, and having visitors. Maybe that's why I've been writing in my diary more often. This afternoon Isaac and Rosemary visited me. I was wondering when they would come and how it would affect Priscilla to see him again. But then it turned out that they missed each other entirely because Priscilla had gone to the store.

Rosabeth is nearly six weeks old now and growing nicely. She seems tiny compared to Dora, but that's understandable. She's sweet and lovable, with a dimple in each cheek and a curl on top of her head. Matthew still runs to "Mammy" whenever he sees me. Hopefully, it will be more frequently now that we live closer to each other.

I enjoyed their visit so much, and I can't imagine that I ever felt so bad that I begrudged them their happiness. When Isaac picked up Dora and talked to her, the corners of her mouth turned down, and I thought she was going to cry, but he put her down then before she started. Rosemary said it seems strange to go to Aunt Polly's house and find that she isn't here. I'm sure of that. Well, it won't be this way long, if my leg heals as it's supposed to.

When Priscilla came home, I told her who was here. She looked startled, but then a smile spread over her face.

"I'm glad he's happily married and has such a good wife," she said in a sincere tone of voice.

I just have to marvel every day over how different Priscilla is from the shallow, flippant girl she was when I first knew her. She cares tenderly for Dora—even changes her diaper—and overall shows a submissive, surrendered spirit. Priscilla seems to be feeling well, but tires very easily. I'm glad there isn't much work to be done, for neither of us could do much. 🌿

November 24, Thanksgiving

*I*s it really only a year since Isaac's wedding day? It seems much longer. So much has happened since then! I received a letter yesterday from Frieda's sister, where Grandma is staying. They want to take a trip to Wisconsin and said Grandma chose to come here over that time, if it's all right with us. That seems too good to be true. I wrote a letter back and urged her to come.

Allen, Polly, and all the children were here for dinner today, also Clyde and Sylvia, and Noah and Eli. Eli's going to be working at home now that Clyde's getting married. Polly prepared all the food and brought it along. She's a good cook, and everything was delicious.

Was it hard for Polly to see someone occupying her house? No doubt it was, but she never let on. She seems to be taking to her new role like fish to the water. She's a kind, motherly soul, and they all seem to love her.

Mary was overjoyed to be able to play with Dora again. When they were ready to leave, Mary begged and begged to be allowed to stay for a few days. Polly looked at Allen, and he said it was all right with him. Mary is a willing little helper and runs errands for Priscilla and me. She also keeps Dora happy and entertained.

I found out that I'm all too human—seeing Allen and Polly driving away together gave me a forlorn feeling. Having Mary here softened my loneliness. She keeps up an almost constant, bright chatter, and it's good for Priscilla, too. Polly brought along most of my clothes and belongings. I'm glad she remembered—and yet it seemed to lessen the tie between me and Allen's family. 🌸

November 25

Grandma came today! Her loving presence is like a holy benediction in this little house. Serene and patient as always, cheerful and joyous. It's nice, too, that Mary can be with her grandma again for awhile. We'll try to respect Grandma's cooking preferences while she's here.

She's amazed by the shelves of good books and expressed her regret that she can't read much anymore because of eyestrain. I offered to read aloud to her, and she accepted gladly. Mary listens quietly, too, even though she probably doesn't understand much yet.

It's snowing tonight, which makes it seem so cozy inside in the warm kitchen. So many blessings to be thankful for! 🌿

November 26

*T*he ground was white with drifted snow this morning, much to Mary's delight—and secretly mine, too. She begged to go out and make a snowman, but none of us was hearty enough to go with her. So she helped make oatmeal cookies and played with Dora.

I started knitting a sweater for Dora, and so Priscilla has taken over the job of reading to Grandma. She read aloud parts of *Pilgrim's Progress* this afternoon, and I found it interesting myself, even though I've read the book before. Every now and then she would stop to ask Grandma a question. What better teacher could she have than her?

I'm glad to hear that Priscilla takes an interest in spiritual matters and has a forgiving attitude toward those who have wronged her. Grandma is a good influence on Priscilla, and their conversations are priceless. Often I lay my knitting aside and jot down Priscilla's questions and Grandma's answers.

Both Grandma and Priscilla are thinking their time on earth may be short, and that creates a special bond between them. The subject is often about dying and resurrection. I think of Grandma as one of God's saints with years of service for the Master to her record. Priscilla I regard as a babe in Christ, but yet still God's child. ❦

This morning Priscilla's mother sent a driver here to pick her up and take her to the hospital. Her dad was rushed there by ambulance early this morning, with all the symptoms of a heart attack.

Rosemary's sister Ruth came over to help us with the children and the cooking while Priscilla was gone. It was a long day for me. I felt weary and restless and heartsick. Over and over I berated myself for not having at least tried to talk to Priscilla's dad about the condition of his soul before it would be too late.

I don't know what I'd have done if Grandma hadn't been here. She spent the day praying—what I was too distraught to do. To distract myself after lunch, I put pillows on the floor for myself, for my leg with the cast, and for Mary and Dora. Then I played with them to their heart's content.

We played pat-a-cake, peekaboo, and hide-the-toy until they were tired. I let them romp over me until Dora fell asleep with her head on my pillow, and Mary climbed on the sofa and soon fell asleep, too. I also took a nap, and slowly the day passed. Finally, at eight o'clock we heard the sound of a car stopping, and Priscilla came in, looking tired and haggard.

"He's gone," she said simply. "He died tonight at five-thirty. It was awful." She covered her face with her hands.

"When Dad realized death was near, suddenly he knew he wasn't ready to die. He realized what a fool he'd been to say there is no God, and that it's all a myth.

"When he realized he'd have to appear before the judgment seat of God, he was in a wild panic and sent someone to bring the ministers as fast as they could. He carried on terribly until they came, saying over and over how sorry he was, and imploring me to forgive him, and crying to God for forgiveness."

Priscilla brushed away a tear and went on, "When the ministers came, Dad told them he had repented and wanted to be saved. Preacher Dan led him to accept Christ and reminded him of the salvation of the thief on the cross. Dad then expressed the wish to join church again, but before he was able to finish the sentence, he took his last breath."

Priscilla wept openly and went to her room to pack some clothes. She's going to stay with her mother over the time of the funeral, and maybe a while longer. Her driver was waiting for her, and after she'd left, I sat there trying to comprehend things.

"Do you really think a deathbed repentance like that is valid?" I asked Grandma.

"That's not for us to say," she replied quietly. "He's in God's hands. I would like to think that God's mercy extends this far.

"But it's risky for anyone to think of putting off repentance until just before death, spurning many chances to repent, continually hardening one's heart. There's a good chance that such a person would have no time or desire before dying to even say, 'God be merciful to me a sinner.' "

*C*lyde and Sylvia's wedding day! Allen sent us word yesterday that he would see to it that someone would pick up Grandma and me in the morning, help us in and out of the house both here and at the wedding, and bring us back in the evening. Isaac stopped in yesterday and said Rosemary offered to babysit Dora. He took Ruth and Dora to their place for the day.

I was undecided about whether I should go to the wedding, with this big cumbersome cast that takes so much room. But Grandma urged me, and so I decided I would. Isaac and Rosemary drove over and got Dora and Ruth early this morning. They'll bring them back tonight. Dora had to cry a little, but I knew she'd be all right as soon as she couldn't see me.

I was all ready and waiting to go to the wedding when I noticed a familiar-looking carriage driving in. Could it really be? Yes, it was Nate's carriage and his sorrel horse! My heart beat fast, and I felt flustered. What could he want?

He tied his horse and came to the door, calling out, "Well, who should I carry out first?"

"Me, me!" cried Mary, and everybody laughed, which eased the tension somewhat.

"Are you taking us to the wedding?" I asked.

"Yes ma'am, if I may have the honor," he said politely. "Allen asked me to bring all of you."

"Okay, you can wheel me out in Grandma's wheelchair," I instructed. "I'll sit on the backseat with Mary so I can stretch my leg."

He boosted me into the carriage and took the chair back to bring out Grandma the same way. Then he folded the wheelchair and put it in the rear carriage box. It was a mild, sunny day, and I found it hard to believe that just last week, snow was on the ground. The air smelled fresh and clean to me after being cooped up so long.

"I didn't even know you were invited to the wedding," I told Nate. "Are you related to Sylvia?"

"Yes indeed! She's my cousin," he replied.

"Is that so? I wonder how long it will take me to find out who all is related to each other in these districts. I'm learning something new all the time."

Suddenly I was struck by the thought that if he was invited, his girlfriend was invited, too! Had he wanted to bring Hannah, but couldn't because of us? That question put a damper on my joy and enthusiasm for going to the wedding.

Nate, however, didn't show any distraction. He was friendly and talkative, and the drive didn't seem long at all. Grandma stood it well, and I decided I'd put the thought of Hannah out of my head and enjoy myself, too.

When we arrived at the wedding, Allen came out of the house to assist us inside.

While Nate was taking Grandma inside, Allen asked, winking at me, "How did you like your chauffeur?"

Hmmmm! What was that wink for? I wonder if he's smitten by Polly's charms and wants to pair off Nate and me. Doesn't he know Nate is going with Hannah? Anyhow, I wouldn't blame him if he has given up on me.

The wedding sermon was inspiring, the ceremony holy and sacred, the meal delicious, and the singing and visiting uplifting. The family decided that Grandma should go home with me again and stay until Priscilla comes back. Mary wanted to go along again, too, and Allen gave permission so she could help care for Dora and run errands.

When we got home to Polly's house, Nate took Grandma and Mary into the house and brought the wheelchair out again for me. For a few moments he just stood there beside the carriage, his ruddy face looking even more red in the glow of the rosy sunset.

Suddenly he said impulsively, "I have a notion to take you along home with me."

As soon as he'd said that, a frightened look crossed his face. I'm sure he hadn't intended to say it aloud.

I laughed unsteadily and quipped, "I wouldn't be able to do much about it, would I?"

After an uncomfortable silence, I added, "I saw you with Hannah on the way home from the hospital. How are things going between you two? Is she still putting you off?"

"No," he replied. "But I'm not happy with her. I tried, but my heart just wasn't in it anymore. . . .

"I can't seem to forget you." His last words weren't much more than a whisper.

"When I saw you and Allen and the children picnicking together that Sunday before your accident, I was sure you belonged together and would soon announce your wedding plans."

So he *was* home that day!

"I dated Hannah a few more times, but there was just no happiness in it. Then when I visited you at the hospital, you seemed so quiet that I felt sure you were purposely discouraging me. Was I right?"

"Oh no! I was just too ill and in pain to hold a conversation."

"Then tell me why you jumped out of the boat so quickly the last time we were together," he said, almost reproachfully.

"Remember the message I gave you from Hannah?" I asked softly. "I didn't want to spoil things between you and Hannah. I figured that if you waited so many years for her, she must be pretty special to you. We were just going together to make her jealous. And I decided, now that she's ready to take you back, it's high time for me to get out of the picture."

"But I called for you to wait," he protested. "Afterward, I must have thought over that little scene a thousand times. The only conclusion I could reach was that you must not have thought much of me, or you wouldn't have run like that." Nate kicked a stone around with the toe of his shoe.

"Oh no! Can't you understand?" I cried. "I cared for you so much that I couldn't stand to stay when I thought you still loved Hannah. I didn't want you to see me cry!"

"Honest?" Nate asked, his face alight with joy.

"Honest!" I confirmed with a smile.

"Well then, may I come to see you on Sunday evening?"

"Yes."

"What will Allen think?" he asked.

"What will Hannah think?" I countered.

He chuckled and replied, "Maybe Allen and Hannah would make a good couple."

After wheeling me in, his parting word was "See you Sunday evening."

My heart is singing. I am so gloriously happy that I can't find words to express it. I'm almost afraid I'll soon wake up and find that it was just a dream. 🌺

*J*oy to the world,
the Lord is come!
Let earth receive her King;
Let every heart prepare him room,
And heav'n and nature sing,
 And heav'n and nature sing,
 And heav'n, and heav'n and nature sing. (Watts)

A happy bunch of carolers were here last night to sing for Grandma and me. I opened the door and the sweet, age-old melodies drifted in the door, along with the frosty winter air. After they stopped singing, I called them inside and Ruth served them hot chocolate and cookies.

They are a nice, friendly, decent bunch, the youth of the church. Mary and Dora loved the attention they received, and Grandma praised them for their good singing and thanked them kindly. Then, calling out their thanks and good-byes, they drove off on their hay-filled wagon pulled by two big workhorses.

Nate, Isaac, Rosemary, Matthew, and Rosabeth were here for dinner. These last few weeks since Priscilla left, Rosemary's sister, Ruth, has been helping with the cleaning, laundry, cooking, and care of the children. With my cast and Grandma's weakness, I don't know how we could have managed without her. She helped me prepare our Christmas dinner of stuffed and roasted turkey, mashed potatoes, gravy, noodles, corn and lima beans, and cabbage slaw. For dessert, we had homemade vanilla ice cream which Nate had turned for me.

When Isaac walked in, carrying Rosabeth, and saw Nate

mashing the potatoes for me, he gave a long, low whistle and said, "What? Henpecked already?"

I liked the answer Nate gave him: "If this is what being henpecked is, then I like it."

As we sat down to the bounteous feast, I thought of the many poor children in the world without food, clothing, and a warm shelter, and the love of kind Christian parents. May we remember to be thankful, and to share with the less fortunate!

This afternoon we visited, talked, sang, shared memories, and played with Matthew, Mary, Dora, and Rosabeth. All too soon it was time for the guests to leave.

I've been thinking all evening: what if I hadn't run off so hastily when Nate didn't want me to? Would we have had a double wedding then, like Isaac suggested? Was it God's will? I've been so happy since Nate chose me, that I didn't even stop to think, Is it God's will?

I was quick to self-righteously tell Allen that I'll do nothing different until God makes his will known. But with Nate I said no such thing. Well, he didn't ask me to marry him (yet?), and I have plenty of time to pray about our friendship and for God's will to be made clear.

I want *his* will to be done, not mine, even if it would mean I can't marry Nate. (I'm trying hard to mean those words!) 🌿

Singing Heart

January 13

*O*h, happy day! My cast was removed at last! If it would be possible, I'd dance a jig around the kitchen. My leg is still weak and needs to be strengthened by exercise.

Ruth entertained Mary and Dora at home while Nate drove me to the medical center and back. I believe he was almost as happy as I was that my leg is healed. He helped me in and out of the carriage. Whatever would I do without him?

Now that I can get around better, Ruth will soon be leaving us. Grandma and I have thanked her repeatedly for helping us through this difficult time.

It was a long three months, but it was worth it, for there were many hidden blessings. "God moves in a mysterious way, His wonders to perform" (W. Cowper). "Jesus, keep me near the cross, There a precious fountain, Free to all, a healing stream, Flows from Calvary's mountain" (F. Crosby). ※

January 17

*W*e received the news today that Priscilla is worse. She spends most of her time in bed, and her mother is caring for her. Grandma and I have been praying for her, and we each wrote her a letter to send with a get-well greeting. I am so thankful for Grandma these days—surely God spared her life because we still need her so much.

Mary will be leaving for home in a few days. I believe it was Polly's doings, but I don't blame her a bit. She wrote a long, cheerful, friendly letter, which I received yesterday. Just by reading between the lines—she didn't really say so outright—I believe she'll be staying there permanently!

She thinks a lot of Allen (and so did I, for that matter), and I know he thinks highly of her, too. If I'm not mistaken, it may be blossoming into a full-fledged romance. Wouldn't that be nice?

My leg is getting stronger, and every day I'm able to do more than the day before. Yet I'll really miss Mary's sturdy little legs and willing nature to do things for me. 🌿

January 22

*T*his morning I enjoyed the drive to church with Grandma, Mary, and Dora. It was a mild day, and we made sure that Grandma was wrapped warmly.

Clyde and Sylvia were in church. I was glad to see them again, even though they swiped Mary from me and took her along to Allen's. I tend to think of Clyde and Sylvia as my son and daughter-in-law, even though I know it's not true.

Nate spent the afternoon here and stayed for supper, but nary a word about marriage has he spoken thus far. Is he missing Hannah after all? Sometimes I think he pays

Dora more attention than he does me. He spent a lot of time with her this afternoon, trying to get her to walk alone, and he nearly succeeded. She's small for her age and fine featured, and seems much too little to be walking.

Now I'll try to write down what I can remember of the sermon. It has been so long since I was able to go to the Sunday meeting. I drank in every word.

In his sermon, Preacher Amos quoted part of Ephesians 5: "Be therefore followers of God, as dear children; and walk in love, as Christ also has loved us and has given himself for us an offering and a sacrifice to God for a sweet smelling savor."

Here are some of his comments: "How are we to walk in love? To walk in the love of Christ, dearly beloved, means to be so filled with Christ's love that he loves others through our lives. The greatest fruit of the Spirit is love. From love come all the other graces. Where love abounds, unkindness and selfishness cannot be present. Love is not easily provoked and does not speak sharply or harshly.

"Many of our enemies could be turned into friends if we loved them with Christ's love, as he loved us. Christ loved us so much, and he showed that love toward us when he held nothing back. He loved us unto the end, and at Calvary he became the perfect sacrifice for our sin. Love is long-suffering.

"If we love with Christ's love, we will not be so upset when someone wrongs us. Instead, let us return good for evil, and freely forgive all. If Christ's love dwells in us, we will not be envious of others' blessings and good fortune, but instead will rejoice with them.

"If any fall into sin or wrongdoing, let us never gloat or look down on them, or delight in gossiping or running them down. Instead, we earnestly pray for them. We hate the sin, but love the sinner. Have we walked even one mile in the other's shoes? We may know nothing of the deep, dark temptations faced, or the feelings of being rejected and unloved by God's people.

"For you were sometimes darkness, but now you are light in the Lord; walk as children of light. One who walks in the light is in daily fellowship with the Lord Jesus. Through the Word of God and daily prayer, we deepen our fellowship with our Savior. Let us be found in Christ, not having our own righteousness, which is of the law, but that which is through Christ, the righteousness which is of God by faith.

"Dearly beloved, notice that it says, Not having my own righteousness. Our own righteousness is as filthy rags in God's sight. Christ is our righteousness. When we are in him, we are covered by his righteousness. We are justified by his grace, through faith. Instead of self-righteousness, we have meekness before God and others.

"As Paul says, the fruit of the Spirit is in all goodness and righteousness and truth. Beloved brothers and sisters, let us be filled and controlled by the Holy Spirit, so we will bring forth the fruit of the Spirit—love, faith, meekness, joy, true humility, peace, hope, and so forth.

"See then that you walk circumspectly, not as fools but as wise, redeeming the time, because the days are evil. Do not allow time to slip away. Instead, grasp it and make every moment count for eternity. Take time to love aright.

"And be not drunk with wine, wherein is excess, but be filled with the Spirit. How can we be filled with the Spirit? We must crucify self and its lusts, confess and forsake all known sin, surrender our life to God, everything and all, heart, mind, soul, and body, holding back nothing. Then God's Spirit will work in our lives as we walk in submission and yieldedness before God. Let us thank God for the true joy that comes from living in obedience."

I believe that Preacher Amos is a man who is close to God. He lives what he preaches and seems to be above reproach. I almost wish I could take notes in church so I could remember all he says. 🌿

February 1

A mild foggy day. Finally we succeeded in making arrangements to visit Priscilla. Grandma wanted to visit her, too, but felt it was too damp to go so far in a carriage, so we got a driver with a van to take us. Nate, Isaac, and Rosemary went along, too.

Priscilla was in a hospital bed in the kitchen. She looks poorly. I have to think of the first time I saw her, at Polly's quilting over two years ago. Then I thought she was fascinating, but soon I found out what a thin veneer that beauty was. *Now* she has beauty of spirit, but is outwardly failing—so pale and colorless, her lips blue, and her hair dry and lusterless.

She seemed glad to see us, but I could tell that it tired her greatly. When Isaac shook hands with her, she said to him, "I am very sorry I treated you the way I did. Will you forgive me?"

Isaac assured her that he had forgiven her a long time ago.

"Please remember me in your prayers," Priscilla whispered to me as I put Dora onto her bed. Dora smiled

137

and wanted to go to her. Priscilla was pleased that she still remembered her, and patted Dora's cheek.

To me, she said, "Kiss Dora, and love her for me. I don't know if I'll ever again be able to care for her."

A tear slipped down her cheek, then she added, "But I know she'll be well taken care of."

And Nate, dear man, told her that he will do all he can to see that Dora is taken care of and properly brought up.

Rosemary squeezed Priscilla's hand and said, "We think of you every day."

But it was Grandma who did her the most good. She and Priscilla have something in common that we healthy ones can hardly share, since we would rather not face our own mortality.

On the way home Matthew sat beside me in the van. Now he is a big boy of three and a half, and somewhat more shy of me, but he still calls me "Mammy"—which still tickles me. 🥀

February 14, Valentine Day

A fat packet came in the mail, containing homemade valentines for us, from Rachel, Dave, Abram, and Mary. There was a letter from each one of them, and also a long letter from Polly. The children all wrote how much they miss me, and "I love you."

I am surprised at how well Mary can print. She had colored a big red valentine and put on it "Be Mine, Sweetheart." Abram's was a large red apple, on which he printed "You are the apple of my eye." Dave's was a colored heart with "2 sweet 2 be 4 gotten."

Rachel had drawn a basket of flowers and printed "Valentine Greetings." I cherished her letter the most. She apologized for being rude when I first came to their place. Next to her mother, she said, I was the nicest person she knew.

I must answer these letters at once. There were messages for Grandma, too, from each of them, and even a valentine for Dora. 🌿

February 19

*N*ate spent this Sunday afternoon here. Grandma and Dora both took long naps, so we had a lot of time to talk and make plans. We decided on Ascension Day, May 4, for our wedding date! The house here is too small to have the wedding. We debated on having it at Nate's place, but then I'd have to spend most of my time there before the wedding, getting ready, so we haven't reached a satisfactory solution yet.

The main topic of conversation after church today was that Hannah has moved to Ohio. She bought a home there and is going to have a fabric store. How nice!

And so I'll be a bride at age forty-two (nearly forty-three)—if we live and the Lord wills. Nate never really asked, "Will you marry me?" like they do in storybooks. Maybe he was afraid I'd react like Hannah did, long ago. But I couldn't have been happier had he worded it any other way.

Half shyly one day he said, "When may I take you along home as my wife?"

Joy seeped out of me like music from happy bells, and

my heart has been singing ever since. For everything there is a season, and a time for every purpose under the heavens: A time to be born and a time to die, a time to plant, and a time to pluck up what is planted. A time to weep, a time to laugh, a time to keep silence, and a time to speak, and last of all, a time to *love!*

Oh, heavenly Father, bless our love, and lead us and guide us. Help me to be like the virtuous woman in Proverbs 31:

Who can find a virtuous woman? For her price is far above rubies. The heart of her husband safely trusts in her, so that he shall have no need of spoil. She will do him good and not evil all the days of her life. She seeks wool and flax, and works willingly with her hands. She is like the merchants' ships; she brings her food from afar.

She rises also while it is yet night, and gives meat to her household, and a portion to her maidens. She considers a field and buys it: with the fruit of her hands she plants a vineyard. She girds her loins with strength, and strengthens her arms. She perceives that her merchandise is good: her candle goes not out by night.

She lays her hand to the spindle, and her hands hold the distaff. She stretches out her hand to the poor; yes, she reaches forth her hand to the needy. She is not afraid of the snow for her household: for all her household are clothed with scarlet. She makes herself coverings of tapestry; her clothing is silk and purple.

Her husband is known in the gates, when he sits among the elders of the land. She makes fine linen and sells it, and delivers girdles unto the merchants. Strength and honor are her clothing; and she shall rejoice in time to come.

She opens her mouth with wisdom, and in her tongue is

the law of kindness. She looks well to the ways of her household, and eats not the bread of idleness. Her children rise up and call her blessed; her husband also, and he praises her. Many daughters have done virtuously, but you excel them all.

Favor is deceitful and beauty is vain, but a woman that fears the Lord, she shall be praised. Give her the fruit of her hands; and let her own works praise her in the gates.

This Scripture is a challenge for me to live with such virtue.

I now feel assured that it is God's will for Nate and me to marry. I've prayed for clear guidance, and although I feel unworthy of such a high calling, I will take the step, in faith. 🌿

March 2

*N*ate came for me this morning with his sorrel horse. We went over to his house to see what I'll have to be getting in the line of furnishings. There was a hint of spring in the crisp morning air, and Nate tucked the carriage robe around Dora. "Warm enough?" he asked. He's so kindhearted. How could I help but love him?

As soon as I walked into the kitchen, I noticed that the wilderness calendars were no longer above the desk, and the hunting-and-fishing magazines were gone, too.

"What happened to your calendars and magazines?" I asked.

Nate looked a little bit sheepish and said, "Hunting and fishing is all right in its place. But I think I carried things a little too far. Now that I'm going to be a married man, I'll put away childish things. So I threw them out and sold all my guns but one. I'll have more worthwhile things to do."

"I admire you for that," I told him. "And it makes me feel like doing my best for you, too, since you're giving all that up just for me."

"I appreciate that," he said warmly. "But it wasn't really just because of you. I was looking at the newspaper, and I saw an obituary of an older man. It said, 'He was an avid hunter and fisherman,' and I thought, What if there would be nothing better to be said about me when I die?

"Then, too, it was just after that sermon when Preacher Amos spoke about making every moment count for the Lord. But don't get me wrong. I'm not giving it up altogether. Hunting and fishing relax me, and as I said, they're all right in their place."

"That sounds wise to me," I agreed.

Nate picked up Dora, and we walked through the rooms of his house to take a look. None of the upstairs is furnished, and it needs a good scrubbing and some fresh wallpaper and paint. I liked the view from the windows, the winding creek, the bridge where the lane crosses the creek, the cows grazing in the meadow, and the big collie dog keeping watch.

The downstairs is sparsely furnished: just the table, chairs, desk, and cupboards in the kitchen. The sitting room has an overstuffed sofa, a chair, and an old-fashioned built-in corner cupboard with glass doors; I have a feeling it's a valuable piece. The bedroom has just a twin bed and a dresser and also needs some fresh wallpaper. The parlor isn't furnished at all.

We sat at the kitchen table, and I made a list of all the

furniture I'd need to find. At the bottom of the list I wrote something just to see what Nate's reaction would be: "Another twin bed for the bedroom." Then I handed the list to him.

His eyes scanned the paper, and at the bottom he took the pencil and crossed out "twin bed" and wrote "double bed."

"Is that all right with you?" he asked anxiously, handing it back.

"Sure," I laughed. "I was just kidding."

He laughed, too. Yet later I thought he was not quite convinced. On the way home he asked me again, "Are you sure you wouldn't rather have twin beds?"

I started to tell him, "Of course I wouldn't," but then I saw him laughing. I was the one being teased and didn't realize it. ❧

March 11

*T*oday after dinner I put Dora in her stroller, and we walked over to Isaac's. It's nice to be able to walk briskly again without limping. Thank you, Lord!

The day was mild and sunny, and I saw the first robin of the season, hopping around looking for worms. My heart always rejoices at seeing the first robin and hearing it sing. It's a reminder that spring will soon be here. When I walked in the lane at Isaac's, to my disappointment I saw that they had hitched a horse to the spring wagon and were ready to go away.

"Hop on!" Isaac called. "We have room for a few more

passengers. We're going to a sale—farm equipment and household items."

I hopped on, and so it happened that I unexpectedly had a chance to purchase some of the furniture I need for our home.

There was a nice, sturdy bureau, several bedroom suites, a sideboard, a hutch, various chairs and rockers, and a breakfast set. Never before had I bid at an auction, and I felt nervous about doing so.

The auctioneer had just put the nicest bedroom suite up for bids, and I wanted it very much, so I made myself brave and raised my hand. I had decided what my limit would be, and the bidding stopped at just a few dollars under that.

The auctioneer cried, "Sold! To the Amish lady with the baby."

I felt embarrassed as all eyes turned toward me, and then, to my consternation, just at that moment I felt someone pulling my purse out from under my arm, where I had tucked it. Quickly I turned around to grab it, because it wasn't even my purse. I had borrowed purse and money from Isaac and Rosemary.

There stood "pickpocket" Nate, laughing at my surprise, and I thought I'd never been so glad to see someone before. He took over the bidding for me, paid for everything, loaded my things on his wagon, and took them along home with him. We even bought a crib for Dora and almost all the other furniture that was there. I found out how handy it is to have along a man with a pocketbook! 🌿

We were at preparatory ser-
vices this forenoon. It was a time of soul-searching, fasting
and prayer, preparing for communion, to be worthy of
partaking of the symbol of Christ's blood shed for us, and
of his body, broken for us.

Right now it's raining and sleeting. What cozy sounds:
the humming of the teakettle on the fire, and the sound of
the sleet against the window panes! Dora is sitting on the
floor, looking at her picture book. Her hair is growing in
curly, which gives her an even more angelic appearance.

Grandma is sitting beside the stove in her rocker, cheerful and contented as always. Never once have I heard her
murmur about her health, lament her lot in life, or com-
plain about not being able to do anything. I know she
spends much of her time praying, mostly for others. I'd
like to impress that scene into my mind so that I never forget it: beloved Grandma in her rocker and one-year-old
Dora playing on the floor.

Thank you, Father, for allowing me to have them both
for this long.

Yesterday I spent most of the day sewing my wedding
dress. There's just a little handwork on the cape to do yet,
then it's finished. I'm so happy, so glad to see it hanging
there beside Nate's new suit, which just arrived from the
tailor.

I must admit that I'm beginning to worry or fret a bit
about where we'll be having the wedding. Nate told me to
pray about it and trust that guidance will be given, and I
want to do that. But I keep forgetting.

I wrote a letter to Polly yesterday and told her of our

plans. If she's not coming back, she may want to put her house up for rent. I'm really wondering how things are between her and Allen. Is she glad I'm not wanting my old job back? Or was she just longing for the day she could move to her own little house again? For Allen's sake, I hope that love and romance will blossom. She would make such a good wife for him, to my way of thinking. ✿

April 4

*S*uch a lovely day! Birds are joyously singing everywhere, and the breeze is laden with the scent of flowers and fields and meadows.

Last Sunday Preacher Amos announced our intentions to be married on Ascension Day, May 4. In the three days since then, we have heard many comments of approval.

Nate has been coming for me every day, and we've repapered the entire second floor. His fifteen-year-old niece, Barbara, helps, too. What a satisfied feeling it gives us when a room is finished, after working hard and doing our best. Next we're going to paint the sitting room and the kitchen.

It feels so good to sit down and rest my aching bones tonight. Some nights I almost kept pasting and hanging wallpaper in my sleep.

This afternoon Nate asked me, "Do you realize that in one month you'll be Mrs. Nathan Mast?"

He nearly startled me. I never heard anyone call him anything but Nate, and the name just suits him. But "Mrs. Nathan Mast" sounds lovely to me, and I told him so.

Then he said, "Miriam Mast, nicer yet."

"Do you really like the name *Miriam,*" I asked in surprise. "It's so plain and old-fashioned."

"It's the nicest name I ever heard," he declared tenderly, "because you're the nicest person I've ever known. I wish I'd have met you twenty years ago."

Oh my, it feels wonderful to be loved! I keep thinking of the verse, She will do him good and not evil, all the days of her life.

Oh God, help me to be all that I should be, to Nate, and all that he thinks I am. ❧

April 11

*N*ate's forty-fifth birthday, and yesterday was Dora's first birthday. I put a birthday card in the mail for his birthday, and I wish I could've seen his face when he opened it.

Today I received a letter from Polly, and I'm sure Grandma wondered what was coming over me when I'd read it. I jumped and danced for joy, an undignified way for an old lady to act.

"I can't believe it," I cried. "Allen and Polly are getting married! They wonder if it's all right if they marry on Ascension Day, too, and we and they can have a double wedding.

"I can hardly wait to talk to Nate about it. He and Polly are cousins, and I have no brothers and sisters and parents to invite, so it really wouldn't make much difference in the amount of people they'd be inviting. And we could share the cost."

We visited Priscilla again on Sunday. She seems to be

holding her own and was glad to see Dora again. Grandma is staying one more week, and then she'll be going to live with her daughter again. We tried to persuade her to live with us (Nate and me), but she decided not to.

Polly wrote that one of her nephews, married last fall, had rented a farm and was planning to move on it. Then just a few weeks ago the owner died and the farm is to be sold, so the deal fell through. She thinks they'd probably be glad for the chance to rent her house. Hopefully, everything will work out all right. I feel so scatterbrained today. Oh Rock of Ages, calm me, and fill me with your ageless peace. 🌿

April 17

*S*pringtime here at Polly's place is wondrous indeed. There are surprises in every corner. I wish I could've spent a summer living here instead of a winter. Out by the blue gate, bluebells, hyacinths, daffodils, and tulips bloom in profusion. The water gurgles invitingly in the brook. In the evening, spring peepers chorus sweetly.

The trees are pushing out green leaves, birds are building nests and joyously trilling their songs to the world, and along the garden, peonies and bleeding hearts are pushing out of the ground. Every day brings something new to see.

Today was Grandma's last day here. This afternoon I was doing some mending and had a chance to have a long talk with her.

"Tell me, what advice can you give me before I step into

the holy bonds of matrimony? I no longer have my mother to ask. Is there anything I should know beforehand? What was it like for you, and what would you do differently if you could live your life over again?"

What she said then, I'll cherish as long as I live. It brought tears to my eyes, so moved was I by her words, although I felt unworthy and undeserving of it.

"I don't need to give you any advice, Miriam. You're following Jesus, you've surrendered your life to him, and you will make a good, virtuous wife for Nate. You will give of yourself, unselfishly, whether it's merited or not, and be like a fruitful vine at his side."

Like a fruitful vine! Those words came as a holy benediction, and I felt that the spot where she was sitting must be holy ground. Tears of joy!

This must be a foretaste of hearing Jesus say, "Well done, good and faithful servant: enter into the joy of your Lord." Her blessing has filled me with a desire to live up to it. I know that self-will and self-seeking far too often take the upper hand.

Oh, heavenly Father, help me to be a fruitful vine in your vineyard, grafted into the true vine, and being constantly filled with your Spirit. 🌿

April 25

*D*ora and I spent the day at Nate's house. Barbara was there helping, too. This forenoon we planted the garden, digging in the rich, black earth, dropping the seeds, and covering them.

Planting always gives me an awesome feeling of being

in company with God. Each seed is a miracle about to unfold! Again, just as we finished, a gentle spring rain began to fall. What a satisfied feeling to know we got the seed in before it rained! Two robins sang with joyous abandon, and my heart felt too full for words.

We sat down to a simple meal of vegetable soup and sandwiches, then walked through the house, inspecting everything. All the rooms upstairs are now furnished—curtains at the windows, quilts on the beds, everything scrubbed and clean. The sitting room is freshly repainted and refurnished, and the kitchen is now painted a light blue over the deep yellow darkened-with-age walls.

The L-shaped kitchen cabinets weren't really old, but they were covered with thick, dark layers of varnish. We removed all the old varnish with Zip-Strip, sanded the bare wood, and put on a light stain and clear varnish. Now it doesn't seem like the same kitchen anymore. *Before*, it seemed rather dark and dingy; *after*, it's light and airy.

A lovely new settee is placed where the old lumpy sofa stood. We worked hard, but it is worth every tired bone and every sore muscle, as Nate said. This afternoon Barbara and I cleaned the sitting room and bedroom downstairs. We also did a quick cleanup job in the empty parlor that Nate said we'll wait till later to fix up.

Before Nate took Dora and me home, we walked around outside. It's so interesting to see what perennials and bulbs are coming up. After we're married, there's still a lot of work for me to do outside, raking and cleaning the yard, spading the flower beds. When I mentioned it to Nate, he said he'd never noticed such things. He thought as long as he got the yard mowed, it was good enough. Sounds just like a man! But, generously, he offered to help me do whatever I think needs to be done.

On the way home, Dora nestled in my arms, fast asleep, long lashes on her exquisitely molded cheeks. Nate looked tenderly at her and said, "I keep thinking that she has a dad out there somewhere. What if he decides, a few years from now, that he wants her? There wouldn't be much we could do about it, would there?"

I stared at Nate for a long moment. Never once had I thought of such a possibility. What if he'd take us to court and make us give her up?

"Let's talk to Priscilla about it," I suggested. "Perhaps she'll agree to have adoption papers drawn up. That way she'd be safe."

"Good idea," Nate agreed. "I'd feel better about it that way."

It gives me a good feeling that Nate is so concerned about Dora and that he accepted her so readily. His worthy character and kindhearted concern are showing freely, and I love him even more for it.

Tomorrow morning Nate is driving us to Allen's, where Dora and I will stay until after the wedding. I'll be helping them to get ready—cleaning, baking, and whatever else needs to be done. I'm really looking forward to working with Polly and being with the children again.

I can not yet comprehend that in just ten days I'll be an old married woman! I keep thinking, What if I had not entered the picture? Would Hannah have this happiness now of becoming Nate's wife?

But then, again, if Joe had not found himself another girl years ago, he probably would have married me. That's just the way life is, it always was, and always shall be, as long as time runs on. Now I'm glad I didn't marry Joe, and

I believe Hannah will someday be glad she didn't get Nate.

For the child of God, all is planned beforehand, and all things work together for good to those who love God.

Precious promises! 🍃

*J*ust seven more days! The whole idea is still so incomprehensible. Me—a married woman, Nate's wife! Becoming one with him for the rest of my life! After so many years of single adulthood, am I ready for such a step? My answer is *yes!* What would I give up in exchange for Nate's love? It's priceless.

I've heard say that marriage is a gamble. Afterward, many are disappointed and wish to be free from the yoke. That's a sobering thought, but I have no doubts about Nate or about our love.

I've enjoyed my week here at Allen's. Polly and Allen are happy—it's plain to see. I am so glad for Allen that I could cry—tears of joy, of course. I doubt that he could've found a better wife anywhere else, had he searched the world over.

Since I'm here, I've been helping to milk the cows every morning and evening; that's something Polly says she can't do. Yesterday morning as we were milking, I said to Allen, "Aren't you glad I broke my leg?"

He laughingly retorted, "Aren't *you* glad you broke your leg? 'God moves in a mysterious way, His wonders to perform' " (W. Cowper).

Noah and Eli painted the barn last week, and it looks a lot better. Rachel helped me clean the attic, basement, and the upstairs rooms in the after-school hours. I was glad for the time alone with her. She's blossoming into young womanhood, a sweet, good-natured girl.

Rachel kept saying over and over how sorry she is that she was rude to me at first when I was here.

I told her, "All is forgiven. We should regret our mistakes and learn from them but never carry them forward into the future with us. When God forgives, he casts the sins into the sea of forgetfulness, and he doesn't want us fishing around in it."

"But I can't believe," she said in amazement, "that you feel the same toward me as you would if I'd never been rude!"

I answered, "I believe I feel even a little more tenderness for you. It showed me how deeply you were suffering from losing your mother. And I rejoiced when the wound began to heal.

"How is it between you and Polly," I probed gently. "Do you think you'll have trouble accepting her as a mother?"

"Yes, I'm afraid I will," she admitted honestly. "But I'll try not to let my feelings control me."

"Put yourself in her place," I suggested. "Treat her as you would want to be treated if you would be in her position. If you act well toward her, your feelings of acceptance will follow."

"I'll try," Rachel murmured.

"And remember, you don't have to do it alone. You have a Savior to whom you can tell all your difficulties, and he will help you gain the victories over wrong feelings." ✺

*P*ear trees are blossoming. What a lovely time of year to get married! The trees and grass and meadows are a lovely green, and spring flowers are blooming everywhere. Buttercups are showing yellow in the lovely, misty meadows, and a flicker is singing its friendly song.

Nate spent the day here at Allen's helping get ready for the wedding. He was so glad to have this opportunity to have a double wedding with Allen and Polly, and he wants to help however he can. Allen had mentioned that the board fence around the meadow should be painted yet, so that's what we were doing all day—he and I and the boys.

Mary is glad for the chance to watch Dora, and a good little mother's helper she is. I was delighted to have the chance to work outside with Nate. Dave and Abram take a liking to him, and it was quite interesting to listen to their conversation.

Abram asked, "Are you a bachelor?"

"That's what they call me," Nate replied.

Dave wondered, "Do you like being a bachelor?"

"Not anymore!" he declared, smiling at me.

Giggling, Abram asked, "Do you like Miriam?"

He chuckled. "Yes, very much!"

Dave quizzed, "Are you glad you're getting married?"

"Yes, very."

"So is Dad," he said proudly.

After that, conversation turned to bunnies and fishing and other things of interest to little boys.

When Nate left for home tonight, I sent along the bowl-and-pitcher set Allen had given me for my birthday. It did bring back memories! So much has happened since then. I can hardly grasp the changes that have taken place.

I'm so glad that Jesus is the pilot of my life. He is at the controls, and he makes no mistakes. 🌿

*P*olly and I were baking cookies most of the day, while Rachel, Mary, and the boys were working outside. It was the first time since I'm here that we were alone and uninterrupted while working together, so we had a heart-to-heart talk. Dora played quietly on the floor.

"Don't you think this is probably creating quite a sensation, really making people talk? Here are two old maids like us getting married, and having a double wedding at that!" Polly said, with that bubbling laugh of hers.

"I'm sure it is," I agreed. "But I've never really felt like an old maid. I still feel like a young girl. Where have those twenty years gone so fast? It's almost as though I went to bed one night at twenty-two and woke up the next morning to find myself forty-two!"

Polly laughed heartily. "You do look young, with not one gray hair, and your slender, girlish form yet. I have gray hair and I'm plump, and that makes me look older. But I don't feel old yet, either. I'm glad Allen has seven children, though, because I'm forty-five years old and won't be able to have any," she said regretfully.

Then she added, teasingly, "You'll probably have half a dozen yet."

I had to laugh in spite of myself. "I do already have

one." I glanced at Dora. "And it would be nice if she could have a sister or brother, or both."

"Isn't it frightening to step out into the unknown future, though?" mused Polly. "We're leaving the safe, secure life we've had."

"Perhaps it's more so for you than for me. Wasn't the thought of giving up your cute little house rather hard?"

"It's like this," Polly replied. "Suppose you had a five-dollar bill in your hand, and someone came along and took it from you, giving you a hundred-dollar bill instead. Would it be hard to give up the five?"

"I wish Allen could've heard you say that!" I exclaimed, with a smile of admiration.

To myself, I reflected, I just hope she'll keep on feeling like that for always. May she always keep on wearing rose-colored glasses. 🍃

April 30

*N*ate drove over after church and spent the afternoon here. I almost wish he hadn't come. A damp, chilly wind has sprung up tonight, and the joy of my hopes and dreams has been dampened, too. Why is it so hard for me to give all my worries and fears to my Savior, to relax and trust that he knows best, that all things will work together for good for us? Is it because I haven't fully given up my self-will yet? I'm afraid so.

Nate and I went for a walk out through the meadow. I was rejoicing in the beauty of the trees and sky and breeze, and was about to comment on it, when he said, "I have something I have to show you." He pulled an envelope out of his pocket, and handed it to me.

The letter was addressed to Mr. Nathan Mast. Inside was a folded piece of paper. I quickly opened it and looked at the signature. Oh no . . . not Hannah again! It was just a note, but a spiteful one—blaming Nate for not keeping a promise he had made to her years ago. The last sentence stated boldly, "You will have to give account of this on the day of judgment, and it will be held against you to your condemnation, let me warn you!"

"What's this about a promise?" I asked Nate, in a puzzled voice.

"I—I should have told you before," he said weakly, kicking at a stone in the grass. "Many years ago I made the promise, and I hoped it wouldn't be valid anymore."

"What did you promise her?" I half whispered, fear clutching at my heart like icy fingers.

"She—I—remember, I told you, four weeks before we were planning to be married, she backed out—told me she wasn't ready after all, to get married. She asked me to promise to wait until she was ready, and never to marry anyone else while she was still single. And I promised to wait until she was ready."

Nate leaned against a tree and covered his face with his hands.

What a blow this was to me. "Do you have any idea what her trouble was?" I finally managed to ask. "Why did she make you promise that, but kept putting you off for so many years?"

Nate blew his nose. "I can't believe I was so blind. She wrote nasty letters to you, and now a letter like this just before our wedding date! All this shows her character rather plainly. It could be that she has some deep-seated emotional problems that were never resolved.

"All the while that I couldn't have her, she seemed desirable to me. But after she asked me to come back, I only began to realize what a selfish, neurotic nature she had. Besides, I was very much in love with you by that time.

"For a long time I wrestled with the question, Would it be all right to break that promise? After I began loving you, I decided that, in this case, it would not be wrong for me to break the promise. I realized it was a rash, foolish promise that I should never have made in the first place. After praying for guidance, I felt that God would forgive me if I didn't keep it.

"Do you think I will be held accountable for it at the judgment day?" Nate asked anxiously.

"Maybe you ought to talk to one of the ministers," I suggested. "I think it was unkind of Hannah to write like she did."

"That's just what I'll do, and right now, too," Nate agreed. "If it wouldn't be so far to bring you back, I'd take you along, too."

Then he left, saying he'd be back on Monday or Tuesday to help get ready for the wedding.

My heart feels sore and rueful. What nerve I had that Sunday I first met Nate and suggested that he pretend he's getting interested in another woman! How foolish of me to meddle in other people's affairs!

Oh God, forgive me! I'm giving all the pieces of my folly to you. Can you make things right, and cause good to come forth from it yet? 🌿

*T*his is Tuesday evening. Thursday is the big day, and Nate has not showed up here at Allen's since Sunday! He told me he would come on Monday or Tuesday to help.

I keep reminding myself, "Why worry when we can pray?" But my foolish heart keeps imagining all sorts of things, and worry grasps my mind like a huge monster.

Has he decided not to go through with the wedding? Did the ministers tell him it would be wrong to break his promise? But why wouldn't he at least come and talk it over with me again?

For over half an hour this afternoon I was pacing back and forth in my room, worrying and praying. Finally I decided that perhaps writing would help to calm me. Now the supper dishes are washed and I am recording my feelings in my journal. My heart mourned privately all day long, but it was not until late afternoon that my anxiety became acute. If only I could somehow reach him by telephone!

How will I be able to sleep? I have a notion to get Mr. Frey to take me to Nate's place, so I can find out what's going on. Meanwhile—I'll cast all my care upon God, for he cares for me.

Oh Father, I give you my fears and worries about Nate. Take care of him, lead him, and give us both wisdom to make the right decisions. Thank you.

 *T*oday was supposed to be our wedding day. But here I am, back in my room in Polly's house, and Nate is far away in the hospital. My eyes keep filling with tears. Why is my life filled with one disappointment after another? But I should be ashamed, thinking only of myself, when Nate is so sick.

Tuesday evening after I wrote in my journal, my anxiety became too much to bear. I walked over to Frey's and, at my request, young Mr. Frey drove me to Nate's place. I took along my suitcase of clothes and this journal, somehow sensing that I wouldn't be returning.

Nate's house was dark, and he was nowhere to be found. It gave me a panicky feeling, and I called loudly, "Nate, Nate, where are you?"

There was no answer, but I thought I heard a moaning or groaning from somewhere outside in the gathering dusk. Then I heard a faint, "Help! Help!" from down by the creek, and there I found Nate lying on the ground.

"Call an ambulance," he said weakly. "I'm terribly sick . . . too weak . . . to move."

I ran as fast as I could to tell Mr. Frey, waiting in his car. He left for the nearest neighbor to call an ambulance. As I tried to fight down my feelings of panic, I slipped into the house and snatched a blanket and lit a lantern to take out to the creek. Then I went back to Nate and tenderly covered him to protect him from the chill.

"When did you get sick?"

"This afternoon . . . I think." Nate could hardly talk.

Tears came to my eyes. Half a day! All alone with no one to help him!

"Food poisoning," he whispered. "I opened a jar of tomatoes for lunch. . . . It smelled a little funny. . . . But the seal was tight. . . . I didn't think it would hurt me. . . . I should have thrown it away." Nate was gasping for breath.

"What if I hadn't come!" I exclaimed, shivering.

I heard an owl hooting in the trees, and something dove into the water with a splash. Then a horrible thought struck me. People have died from food poisoning, even with expert care given right away. What if Nate is so far gone that they can't save him?

It seemed like a long, long time until finally I saw the blinking lights of the ambulance, coming in the lane. What a relief! The emergency crew worked over Nate to help him breathe. Then I went along to the hospital and spent the night in the waiting room. In the morning they came and told me Nate was still very sick from botulism but out of danger. The nurse advised me to go home and get some sleep.

I did remember to call Frey's to send Allen the message that they were to go ahead and get married this morning without us, and why. Today, instead of being at their wedding—or at *our* wedding—I was visiting Nate in the hospital.

Has such a thing ever happened to anyone before? It seems to me I heard of a couple that had been published for a whole year before they got married. Will we ever get married? I am too tired to think tonight.

Oh, God, heal Nate and make him well, according to your will. 🌿

*T*hings happened pretty fast here today. Nate came home from the hospital this forenoon, and I went over to welcome him home. I brought in the mail for him: the mailbox was filled with get-well cards, which he told me to open and read aloud to him.

In the second envelope was another letter from Hannah! This time she was apologetic and friendly. She heard that we hadn't gone through with our wedding plans, but hadn't found out why. Apparently she thought it was because of her other letter, and her conscience smote her.

Hannah wrote that she was sorry, that she'll forgive Nate and release him from his promise, and that we are to go ahead and get married.

"Hmmmm. She must be made of pretty good stuff after all," I told Nate. "That sure was nice of her."

"Let's get married today yet," Nate said impulsively. "I want you to stay and help me get well."

"Do you think it would be possible?" I gasped.

"Why not? We have our marriage license, and we were published three weeks ago. All we need is the bishop and a few witnesses. Could you get word to Allen and tell him and Polly to come and bring Bishop Dave along? And Isaac's, too?"

"Do you really want me to try?"

"Yes, please do," he pleaded. "After being alone those nights when I was so sick, I have the horrors of being alone again."

And so, several hours later, Nate's bedroom was filled with people—Isaac and Rosemary, Allen and Polly, Bishop Dave, and Preacher Dan.

Nate was too weak to stand. Dan and Dave each had a short sermon. Then we propped up Nate with pillows in the bed, and we went through the ceremony of being joined in holy matrimony. It was different, but now we *are* husband and wife!

The day was tiring for Nate. He fell asleep as soon as the people left and is still sleeping. He has lost a lot of weight, and I'm so glad I can be here to nurse him back to health.

Now I think, Maybe it *was* God's plan that it should happen this way. At least Hannah had a change of heart because of it. We won't have much of a normal honeymoon, but I praise and thank God for his blessings and guidance.

Allen's brought Dora along for me, and Mary wanted to stay, too. I'm glad for her: she can help to entertain and watch Dora. They're playing out in the yard, and I must go and prepare a bite of supper for us. ✿

May 15

I never realized how beautiful springtime could be here among the trees and along the creek. We wake up to a lovely chorus of birdsong and fall asleep to the poignant croaking of the bullfrogs.

Nate is slowly getting better. At first he wasn't able to eat and had no appetite. The doctor said it will take time and that it's a miracle he's alive.

I had visions of cooking good, rich meals for him, and in no time he would be strong and robust again. But now broths and liquids are about all he can tolerate. The neighbors are kind and helpful, doing the necessary farm work for Nate.

Isaac and Rosemary have often been over, and she and I were working in the neglected yard. I can't believe how much better it looks! We picked up twigs, raked and mowed, and spaded the flower beds. She's bringing me a flat of impatiens tomorrow, and we'll put them in as shade-loving plants here under the trees. We hoed the entire garden while Mary, Matthew, and Dora played nearby and Rosabeth sat in her jumper.

This is a precious, hallowed time for me—feeling the loving concern of the neighbors. I hope we can do the same for them as the need arises, especially for Isaac and Rosemary; they helped more than anyone else. Nate sat outside in the sunshine for a while this afternoon, on a carriage blanket, while the children romped around him. After Isaac's left, I joined him there.

"Our first week of marriage has been quite different than we'd planned it to be, hasn't it?" Nate said quietly.

"At least we're together," I replied. "I don't think I could bear it not to be with you and take care of you."

Dora came toddling up to me, then, with a tulip in her hand, and held it up to me. What is sweeter than a little girl with a flower? I hugged her and thanked her, then gave the flower back to her and said, "Give it to Dad."

She walked right over to Nate, said "Dad" clearly and distinctly, and handed the tulip to him.

It was nearly too much for Nate, and he wiped away a tear. "God has been good to me," he murmured huskily.

My own heart is too full for words. ❧

*N*ate is feeling good again, and about as hungry as a bear just out of hibernation. At last I can cook to my heart's content. Mary and Dora are inseparable, and it's so nice that they can play outside. With Mary watching, I don't have to worry that Dora will get too close to the creek and the waterwheel.

Yet in the afternoon when Dora is taking her nap, Mary needs something else to do. I wish I could persuade Allen and Polly to let us adopt Mary, but I know it would be useless even to try. This afternoon Mary said she wants to make cookies while Dora sleeps. So I got out the necessary ingredients and helped her to measure them, while Nate watched from the recliner.

"Maybe you should be the one teaching her now," I said to Nate. "You were doing your own cooking for quite a while."

"Ever since Mother died. And I poisoned myself, so that proves it was high time I got a cook," he chuckled.

"What was your mother like?" I wondered. "Was she good-natured like you?"

"She was kind, almost as good as you. But she could hardly get around anymore. Her hip became crooked in her old days, and she was bent forward from the waist and couldn't straighten up."

"Poor woman. She must have been a good mother, to raise a son like you. And your dad . . . describe him to me, too. I wish I could have known them both."

"People always told me I looked and was just like him," Nate replied. "Of course, *I* didn't think so."

"Like father, like son," I mused. "That gives me hope

that we'll have a son who looks and is just like you." I smiled at Nate.

"How about a daughter that looks and is just like you?"

Back came his answer: "I'd like that, too." 🌿

*T*his was our first Sunday in church together as a married couple, and many spoke to wish us God's blessing. Today we've been married one month, and this week I'll be forty-three years old.

As I look back over the years of my life, I see my failures and weakness and waywardness. Yet I thank God for his grace through Christ to cleanse my heart again. Yes, there has been loneliness and heart hunger, but the love of God has always been there to fill that emptiness inside. His love is so deep and wonderful, his joy is above any earthly joy, and his peace passes all understanding.

Being one with Christ, grafted into the true vine, and filled with his Spirit—this far surpasses any earthly union. I now realize that during all my years of singlehood, I had the false idea that marriage surely spells true happiness. When someone got married, I even made such remarks: "She deserved happiness," or "I'm so happy for him."

I was contented when I accepted my lot in life, but I had an idea that marriage would be instant supreme happiness. Now I realize that, while other human beings may bring us happiness, that joy is transient. In a moment, our marriage partner could be taken from us.

Without the love of God and union with Christ and the church, what would we have? Friends may desert us, love may grow cold, human help may be scarce—and if we had not the Lord and his people, what would we have? That is a wise exhortation, to "seek your happiness in the Lord."

Our life should be a step-by-step, day-by-day walk with Christ in obedience and yieldedness, a stepping heavenward, ever striving for closer fellowship with the Lord, and getting closer to him as we journey homeward. This fellowship and oneness with him is the greatest thing any human can have, the only thing that can fill the emptiness inside and bring true fulfillment.

And anyone, married or single, who sincerely comes to Christ, may be partaker of his abundant life. Let the one who is thirsty come. And let whosoever will, take of the water of life freely. 🍃

June 17

*R*ose and honeysuckle time again! I have a bouquet of roses on the kitchen table, and it perfumes the whole room. Tonight Nate and I and the children sat outside in the yard, watching the dusk descend. The peace and beauty of the evening was like a sweet benediction.

Fireflies flickered everywhere, and Mary and Dora ran around trying to catch them. Watching the flashes of light in the trees along the creek brought back memories of boating with Nate, and I had a sudden longing to go for a boat ride again. Nate agreed, and we carried the boat out of the shed and down to the water.

"Let's hope this is a happier ride than the last one was, when you ran off from me!" Nate exclaimed. "That was the last time I had the boat in the water."

"I'm sorry now. But all's well that ends well, not so?"

Mary and Dora came running, and we tied life vests onto them. We settled on the seats, and Nate manned the oars. Night insects were singing, frogs were chorusing, and an occasional bird twittered in the trees.

Nate rowed silently except for an occasional splash of an oar as it hit the water. Mary and Dora snuggled against me, half afraid of the darkness and water. Such loveliness and tranquillity surrounded us, and it was too awesome for words.

Thank you, Father, for the beauties of nature that hallow and enrich and beautify our lives. 🌿

July 8

*M*ary is at home again now, and we all miss her. We finally got around to visiting Priscilla again. She has gone backward since we last saw her and is thin and pale. We broached the subject of adopting Dora, but Priscilla didn't seem interested.

"God will protect her from evil," she declared. "Besides, I believe I'm going to be healed, and then I'll want Dora back."

"Oh?" I had a sinking feeling in my chest. "Have the doctors found a cure for you?"

"Oh, no." She held up a book entitled *Jesus, Our Healer.* "I'm taking Jesus as my healer," she stated simply. "Jesus Christ, the same yesterday, today, and forever. He healed many people while he was still on earth, and he is still the same today."

"Yet there is a time appointed for each of us to die," Nate reminded her.

"If Jesus heals me, then I will live," she said quietly.

"I think we should seek God's will in the matter," Nate cautioned.

"Oh, but it is God's will to heal!" Priscilla insisted.

We changed the subject then, and Priscilla asked us to lift Dora up on the bed. She shyly clung to me, and Priscilla said, "Come sweetheart, come to Mamma."

A strange pain filled my breast. I had just begun to teach Dora to call me Mamma since I'm married, and now this!

"I think it's time for us to be leaving," Nate said then, much to my relief. "We have a long drive home."

On the way home we discussed Priscilla's newfound beliefs. "I know it's cruel of me to wish she wouldn't recover," I confessed. "But I haven't yet been able to find it in my heart to be willing to give up Dora."

Nate tweaked Dora's nose. "I can't believe it would be God's will for Dora to go back to an unstable single mother, when with us she could have a good mother like you."

"You mean a good kind dad like you," I corrected him.

"Let's pray about it," Nate suggested, "and ask for God's protecting hand over her, and for his guidance. He makes no mistakes and does all things well."

That's a comforting thought. ❧

July 23

Going to church here in this district is a time of soul-satisfying fellowship for me. Just one thing mars my happiness. Every time, as today, Mamie

Lapp comes to me, takes my hand, and wants me to sit beside her.

I tell Mamie I'm sorry, but I have to sit in the women's section now. Poor soul! She takes it as personal rejection, wipes away tears, and walks off. She always hopefully tries again the next church Sunday. I wonder if anyone would object if I'd invite her to sit with the married women.

We spent the afternoon down by the creek, spreading carriage blankets on shaded grass and a few pillows for Dora when she naps. We regard her with a new tenderness now. Before our last visit with Priscilla, I never had any fears that we might be asked to give her up, but now the thought is never far away.

Nate talked of his boyhood days and his younger years, his hopes and dreams and ideals. Years of loneliness, self-denial, soul struggles, failures, victories, and peace. I believe his hard life has helped to form the worthy character he now has, and I thank God for the peaceable fruit of righteousness.

Lying in the sunshine that filtered through the leaves on the trees above, I wondered, as I so often have, how it is that I've been given a husband like him to love. Lord, help me to be worthy of his love. 🌿

August 2

*T*here's a warm south wind tonight, and the windmill is whining and creaking in the wind. I've grown to love that sound since I'm living here. Also, the music of the wind through the trees, the sound of the waterwheel down by the creek, and the crickets chirping. How dear everything is here! I feel secluded from life's calamities, from wicked people, from fear, discouragement, and from anything bad. Here I'm surrounded by the sacredness of love, wonderful love.

Dora is asleep in her bed, and there is Nate now, coming in from the field with the horses. It's almost too dark for me to see him, but I can hear him whistling as he unhitches the horses, and soon he will join me here on the veranda.

Just today we heard that in October a new preacher will be ordained by lot for this district! As soon as I heard it, a queer feeling caused butterflies in my stomach. Oh, what if it would be Nate? In September, one of the two preachers, Dan or Amos, will be ordained bishop.

This district has been without a bishop for awhile, and it's becoming too much for Bishop Dave to handle both his district and this one. I'm sure that it weighs heavily on the minds of the eligible men and their wives. We'll all be praying about it.

Nate is walking in now, so I'll lay my diary aside. 🌿

O that we would praise the Lord for his goodness and for his wonderful works to the children of men! What a wonderful thing it is to feel well!

I just came back from taking a short walk with Dora. The earth was freshly washed after yesterday's rain, and I gazed in awe at the lovely pink roses blooming in the garden, and the beautiful blue sky above me. A mockingbird was singing, and the air was fresh and invigorating.

After being sick for what seemed like such a long time, it seems too good to be true to feel good again. And I am hungry and can eat without being nauseated. I'll never take good health for granted again, I hope.

Now that I'm feeling well again, I'm beginning to feel happy and excited. The price of motherhood is high, but well worth it. Nate has been kind and sympathetic and helpful, doing most of my work for me while I was unable to do it. This is a lot more bearable because of how he is cheerfully taking care of me. Nate is so thoughtful and compassionate.

I keep thinking of that upcoming ordination. What a wonderful preacher Nate would make! I've told him of my feelings about it, and he's not the least bit worried. He just shrugs it off and says he doesn't believe he'll be in the lot. He's certainly not losing any sleep over it. I wish I could be so nonchalant about it.

Mmmmmm! The kitchen is filling with the wonderful aroma of the vegetable-beef noodle soup that is simmering on the stove. I'm hungry! 🌿

*W*hat an enjoyable afternoon this has been! Rosemary, Matthew, and Rosabeth were here for a few hours. It's good to have another woman with whom to talk and share experiences. I noticed that Matthew no longer calls me Mammy, but I don't mind. Rosabeth is toddling around by herself now, and she's nearly the same age Matthew was when I first started working for Isaac. Time sure flies.

Rosemary told me that Priscilla has taken a sudden turn for the worse. She is in the hospital and in critical condition. As a last-ditch attempt to save her life, they're going to try a new drug on her, one that could have serious side effects and will either kill or cure.

Oh, God, help me to give up my own selfish will in the matter. Help me to pray for her healing, if it's your will, and mean it. How can I be so heartless? What if *I* would be on my deathbed, wanting to live to raise my daughter?

Heavenly Father, you know what's best for little Dora. I give her into your hands. If my giving her up is best for her, then I consent to it. 🌿

*T*he ordinations are now history. Preacher Amos is the new bishop. Four men were in the lot for ordaining a preacher, and three walked out free of the burden. Only one, and that was Isaac, walked out with the weight of the full responsibility on his shoulders.

My heart goes out to him and Rosemary. So young! I

wonder, Is that why he had to endure all the trials and disappointments he went through, to prepare him for the work ahead? A poet once said, "Ah! must Thou char the wood ere Thou canst limn with it?" (F. Thompson).

That feeling I had on the lot, it must have been for Isaac instead of Nate! But really, I think it's a good indication that feelings are undependable.

We prayed for the Lord's will to be done. During the ordination the suspense of waiting and not knowing was heavy, as Bishop Amos and Bishop Dave set out the hymnals. Only one contained the slip of paper on which was written a Bible verse: "The lot is cast into the lap; but the whole disposing thereof is of the Lord."

The suspense mounted as each man in the lot chose a book. Then, one by one, Amos searched for the paper and, not finding it, handed it back. Isaac was the youngest, and since it hadn't been in any of the other hymnals, it had to be in Isaac's. Many were moved to tears as Bishop Amos ordained him, and said, "May God bless you, and may you consecrate your whole life to his divine service."

Many a prayer rose to the throne above in Isaac's behalf, and also for Rosemary. My own spirit felt light as we drove home. Yet my whole heart goes out to them. I want to do all I can to make it easier for them, for now they carry the burden. 🌿

October 29

With a feeling of awe and amazement, I witness the changes within my body—the first faint flutterings of life and movement!

My attitude has been one of disbelief: Can it be true that I'm to be a real mother, not just a substitute one? But it's different now that I have tangible proof. Before this I kept telling myself, Don't get your hopes too high. Maybe it's not really true at all. Yet the miracle, though unseen, is happening.

Nate is protective of me, constantly cautioning me not to overdo or lift too heavy, and wanting to help me all he can. If he's already like this now, what will he be like a few months from now? It certainly makes me feel loved and cared for.

The trees along the creek are gorgeous with reds and golds and browns. I don't believe I've ever seen them so lovely before. My heart rejoices to see God's handiwork thus displayed. How good it is of him to give us such beauty! Let everything that has breath praise the Lord! 🌿

November 30

We visited Priscilla again today, and the new drug seems to be working. She's at home, and up and around.

I expected to see her happy, rejoicing, and praising God, but instead she was upset. She claims the drug was given to her against her wishes. She wanted to be healed without any earthly means, just entirely by Jesus. She's sure he would have healed her without any drugs or doctor. I tried to explain to her that God uses the doctors as a channel for his healing, but she didn't agree.

I had a few words alone with her mother before we left, and she said that Priscilla is definitely not out of the woods yet. Her medicine makes her feel irritable and hard to please. Thankfully, nothing was said about Dora. We had dropped her off at Ben Esh's, not knowing whether Priscilla was well enough to see her.

How dear Dora seems to me tonight, playing with her toys on the floor, and every now and then coming over to me to baby-talk and to show me something. Babies change so fast. I'm trying to impress the picture of her in my mind: her heart-shaped face, yellow dress, and dark curls.

Just now she came over to me with her doll, and said, "Mama, hold me."

She calls us Mama and Daddy now, which thrills us both. As long as there's a breath of hope, we'll keep on hoping and praying that she can stay with us, if it be God's will. 🌿

December 25, Christmas Day

*W*e spent a quiet day at home. I've been thinking about Grandma a lot these days. Is she well? I think I'll write her a long letter. She's been such an inspiration to me.

It's cozy inside today, with the wind howling around the corners of the house and through the swaying trees outside. Nate is down on the floor, romping with Dora, and they're both enjoying it immensely. Will we be able to keep her?

I'm thinking back to other memorable Christmases. There is gladness and joy in my heart for God's unspeakable gift of his Son to this sinsick world, that we might be redeemed and cleansed, so we can strive to be a fruitful vine in his vineyard.

YEAR FIVE

Together

January 14

*T*oday we were at Dr. Wing's office for my seventh-month checkup. He told me that I definitely am carrying twins!

In the midst of my excitement, I thought he seemed rather grave, so I asked him, "Is something wrong?"

He quickly replied, "No, everything's fine, but having a first baby at your age is risky, and having two could further complicate matters."

At the time I was so happy and excited that I hardly heard what he was saying, but since then, I've been thinking about it. Well, I won't let it worry me, for everything is in God's hands, and he makes no mistakes.

Finally we're having snow, real snow instead of flurries. I love to see the earth covered with the pure white stuff.

Wash me, and I shall be whiter than snow. ※

February 27

*O*nly a few more weeks of waiting! The housecleaning is all finished, thanks to niece Barbara's help. I've done a lot of baking ahead. Now that I'm all ready, time seems to crawl.

These days Dora is so active, a good pastime for me. In the shop Nate is busy making two little beds.

I'm half afraid there'll be a big snowstorm just when I'll have to go to the hospital. I wanted a home delivery, but Dr. Wing wouldn't hear of it. He said, "Perhaps if you'd be twenty-three instead of forty-three, I'd allow it." So I guess I'd better take his advice.

During these last weeks, I'm feeling bodily heaviness, but lighthearted joy. I can hardly wait! ❧

March 12

I'm lying here in bed, by turns writing in my journal and gazing at cute little Peter. On the morning of March ninth, we went into the hospital, and at 12:45 baby Peter was born. A few minutes later baby Amanda arrived. She weighed a few ounces over five pounds, and he weighed six pounds.

Nate was allowed in the delivery room, and being there together with our babies was one of the happiest times of our lives. Who can find words to describe the awesome miracle of birth? To have two perfectly formed, healthy-looking babies given to us seemed incomprehensible.

However, we came home this morning with only Baby Peter. To leave without Baby Amanda was almost more than I could bear. She has been identified as having *glutaric aciduria*. It's new to me, but Nate said he knows of several families with children who have it.

Thanks to a dedicated doctor who studied this problem among our people, there is hope she can lead a fairly normal life. She needs to be on a low-protein diet. The doctors have been reassuring, but my state of euphoria has been replaced by gnawing fear. I want to have her home.

Nate has been comfortingly strong. What would I do without him to lean on? 🌿

*M*y heart is full of wonder and thankfulness as I gaze on my two sleeping babies. To have them both here together seems to be too wonderful to be true.

Amanda has dark, wispy hair, well-shaped features, so amazingly dainty and sweet. Peter looks just like Nate. He even has hair that shines a bit red. Both are adorable, sweet, and cuddly. Can it really be true?

Dora seems to be fascinated by the babies. She spends a lot of time standing by their cribs, watching them, sometimes reaching in to softly stroke their hair.

What a lot of care two babies take! But I'm cherishing every moment: rocking them, feeding them when they're hungry, changing diapers. Nate helps a lot, and Barbara is doing the housework.

Precious, unforgettable days! 🌿

I'm trying not to worry about Amanda. I've been hearing more about glutaric aciduria from other families. I had a letter yesterday from a mother whose daughter has it, is paralyzed, and lacks muscle control. Thanks to medical research, the disease can now be treated before the symptoms strike, and actually prevent the symptoms. Do I have this right? It still all seems so new to me.

Bringing children into the world is such an awesome responsibility.

Oh, God, help me to be a good mother. I feel weak and overwhelmed.

Do I have a case of postpartum blues? 🌿

April 5

*H*appiness is:

Nate sitting on the rocking chair with a baby in each arm, trying to get a smile out of them.

Having a bouquet of lovely daffodils and sweet-smelling hyacinths in a vase in front of me.

Taking a walk down to the creek with Dora, in the lovely springtime.

Being able to see my toes again, without bending over.

Hearing a robin joyously singing in the tree outside the open window.

Finding Dora fast asleep beside Amanda in her crib, with an arm around her, and her cheek pressed against hers.

Seeing Nate out in the field, riding the sulky plow behind his team, turning over the rich, black earth in neat, long furrows.

Getting a long letter from Polly and Allen.

Having a visit from Isaac and Rosemary and the children.

Feeling the prayers of the brothers and sisters in the faith, and knowing the goodness of God. 🌿

May 11

*O*ur first anniversary. It's been a happy year, and our love has grown stronger and deeper. Illness and pain have been forgotten, and we are enjoying the babies. They are both thriving, but Peter is growing faster than Amanda. She has a placid disposition, while he tends to be more fussy.

Already I can hardly imagine what life was like without them. I became a mother at almost exactly the same age my mother was when she had me. Ordinarily that wouldn't seem like much of a coincidence, but we were the age many women are when they become first-time grandmothers!

I have found peace, both about Baby Amanda's condition, and about whether or not we'll be able to keep Dora. We have a loving heavenly Father, and even though he does not always give us what we want, we can rest assured that he gives us what is best for us.

God is all-knowing and all-wise, and someday we'll understand the whys and wherefores of his perfect plan for us. Trust in the Lord with all your heart. In all your ways acknowledge him, and he shall direct your paths. 🌿

May 24

*T*here are only a few pages left in my journal, and next time we go to town, I want to get another one. I feel an inner urge to write down thoughts, happenings, feelings, and sometimes prayers.

I've decided to give this journal a title, "A Fruitful Vine." My thought is not that I've brought forth much fruit, but that life has yielded abundantly for me, and thus far it has been fruitful and rewarding. I am grateful for all of God's blessings.

There have been loneliness, sorrow, and heartache, but the Lord has been with me through it all. His promises never fail. If I would not have had to go through hard times, I wouldn't have learned to trust God in adversity. The knowledge that he carried me through rough ways is precious to me. And because of that memory, I can appreciate the good times more.

The next journal will be an important one, for hopefully it will be filled with the joys of caring for our little family. Baby talk, bundles of joy, first smiles and steps and words, and much more. I hope to be able to write that we could adopt Dora, and that she is now our daughter.

I've been debating what title I want to give the next journal. I thought perhaps, "A Peaceful Stream," but no, who knows how peaceful the future will be? So I decided on "A Winding Path." I know the future won't be all straight paths, for life has many pitfalls and hindrances and stepping-stones.

I don't know what the future holds, but I know that my Savior has said, "I will never leave you nor forsake you." So even though the path is winding, I won't have to walk alone. Happiness is neither within us or without us; it is in the union of ourselves with God, who will lead us by the hand to our heavenly home.

Scripture References

YEAR ONE

July 28: Ps. 18:30; John 3:16; Num. 6:24; John 6:44; Deut. 31:6; Heb. 13:5; Jer. 8:22.

July 29: Ps. 27:11; 139:23-24; 143:8; 40:8; Mark 14:36.

Sept. 2: 2 Cor. 13:9.

Sept. 7: Matt. 25:1-13; Eph. 5:25-27; Rev. 19:8-9; 21:2, 9; 22:17; Eph. 4:30.

Oct. 15: Ps. 121:1-2.

Nov. 5: 1 Pet. 5:7.

Nov. 7: Matt. 18:22.

Nov. 14: John 15:4-7; 1 John 2:5-6; Rom. 8:28; 1 Cor. 6:19; 1 Thess. 5:17.

Dec. 28: Luke 2:1-18; Matt. 2:1-22; 4:16; John 1:9; Matt. 10:8.

YEAR TWO

Apr. 19: Rev. 7:17; 21:4.

May 17: Eph. 5:1-2; Gal. 5:22-23; Matt. 5:44; Rom. 12:21; James 3.

Sept. 1: Isa. 61:10; Rev. 19:8; 21:3-4.

Oct. 20: Ps. 51:1-2.

Nov. 26: Prov. 3:5-6

Dec. 12: 1 Thess. 5:17.

YEAR THREE

Jan. 1: Phil. 3:13-14.

Jan. 16: Rom. 8:28.

Mar. 9: Ps. 51:17; Eph. 2:8-20; Matt. 16:24; 18:18-20; Rom. 3:23; 6:23; John 6:44, 37; 1 John 1:9; Prov. 28:13; John 1:12; 3:16; Tit. 3:5.

Apr. 15: Song of Sol. 2:12.

May 10: 1 Cor. 2:9.

June 16: Job 7:6; James 4:14; 1 Cor. 15:52.

July 1: John 15.

Aug. 29: Prov. 22:6.

Sept. 22: Heb. 12:11; Phil. 4:7; John 14:27.

Oct. 16: Phil. 4:7.
Nov. 3: Ps. 46:10.
Nov. 16: 1 Cor. 15:31.
Nov. 30: Luke 23:39-43; 18:13.

YEAR FOUR
Jan. 22: Eph. 5; Gal. 5:22-23; 1 Cor. 13:5; John 13:1; Rom. 12:21; Eph. 5:8; Phil. 3:9-10; Isa. 64:6; Eph. 5:9, 15-16, 18.
Feb. 19: Eccl. 3; Prov. 32:10-31.
Mar. 19: 1 Cor. 11:23-29.
Apr. 4: Prov. 31:12
Apr. 17: Matt. 25:21.
Apr. 25: Rom. 8:28-29; Ps. 139.
May 2: 1 Pet. 5:7.
June 11: Phil. 4:7; Rev. 22:17.
July 8: Heb. 23:8; 9:27; Mark 7:37.
July 23: Heb. 12:11.
Sept. 16: Ps. 107:15.
Oct. 15: Matt. 6:10; Prov. 16:33.
Oct. 29: Ps. 150:6.
Dec. 25: 2 Cor. 9:15.

YEAR FIVE
Jan. 14: Ps. 51:7.
May 11: Prov. 3:5-6.
May 24: Ps. 128:3; Josh. 1:5; Heb. 13:5.

The Author

The author's pen name is Carrie Bender. She is a member of an old order group. With her husband and children, she lives among the Amish in Lancaster County, Pennsylvania.